MADAME VAMPIRE

by Robin Burks

The Romanian swayed back and forth, her mouth opening and closing, saying nothing.

My mother's patience ran out as she tightened her grip and shook the old woman.

The Romanian took a deep breath and uttered a single word, her voice barely above a whisper. "Mullo."

My mother shook the woman again.

The Romanian spoke once more, this time in French. "Vampyr," the crone hissed as she crossed herself three times and tried to break from my mother's grasp.

I listened and observed from where I lay.

My mother growled. "How do I save her? How do I save my daughter?"

Tears formed in the Romanian's frightened eyes. The old woman answered, but her voice shook as she muttered, "Blood, she needs blood."

Something settled upon the room, as if warmth descended upon us with the truth. My mother let go of the woman and smiled.

The Romanian walked away as if to leave, but my mother grabbed her by her long hair and yanked her back.

"Then blood she will have," my mother replied calmly as she pulled a small knife from the bodice of her dress and cut the woman's throat.

The Romanian gurgled as blood poured from the wound. Something awoke in me, strange and sweet, as the coppery scent of blood filled the room. I felt a longing as hunger rose within me. I finally understood all.

My mother shoved the Romanian on the bed, where the old woman landed in a bloody heap on my ivory lace sheets.

"Drink," my mother said.

CHAPTER ONE

The story of my life is written in blood. It is a long tale, for I have lived a long life, but I fear that my time grows short. Even now, a shadow follows me, bringing with it *le morte*. If I die, let it be known that I lived. I am Jeanne "Reinette" Antoinette Poisson, Madame de Pompadour, mistress to a king, marquise and vampire. I have killed many. I regret *rien*, nothing.

When I say that I am a vampire, I do not mean that I am like those creatures one might see in a modern novel, in a film or on television. I do not fear the night and often enjoy long walks on sunny days. I can even admire my lovely reflection in mirrors. Wooden stakes cannot kill me, but other simpler things could prove dangerous. I also do not possess the ghastly sharp teeth often attributed to my kind, nor do I fear the sign of the cross.

But I get ahead of myself. I was born Jeannette Poisson in the year 1721, four days after Christmas, to a woman I learned to love, admire and fear Madeleine de La Motte. I never knew my real father, or who he was, and it's likely that my mother wasn't sure of his identity either: she was a wild thing, always caught up in one torrid affair after another. However, I often liked to imagine that I was born immaculately, much like the beloved Virgin Mary, having emerged from my mother's untouched womb covered in blood and embryonic fluid.

Several men claimed parentage to me, especially after my rise in the French court, but my mother would not admit to being involved with any of them. There was one, though, who treated me as if I were one of his own, and that was Le Normant de Tourneham, but I only mention him now in passing.

As a girl, I was a pale and sickly thing, I often suffered from horrible fits of illness that left me bedridden for days and made me weak and frail. I never possessed much of an appetite for food or drink and only indulged in such things as expected of me. I could not play or do other things that children did, for even the least strenuous of childhood activities depleted what little strength I had.

My physicians believed that my time on Earth was short and told my mother I would not survive to see my 10th birthday.

I grew weaker with each passing day and by my eighth birthday, I could not even rise from my bed. I began to spend all my days staring at the ugly yellow canopy above me as the overbearing scent of orange and bergamot did little to hide the odor of my illness and inevitable death.

My mother, who was always a superstitious woman, brought in priests to pray over me, but my condition never changed. Desperate, she turned to the more arcane arts after meeting a Romanian woman on the Rue de Rivoli. After my mother explained my affliction, the Romanian promised she could help me. In return, my mother promised her, a woman who was no more than a beggar, a warm meal and coin.

Mother brought this woman into our house and showed her where I lay. I could barely lift my head to look up, but I saw the Romanian out of the corner of my eye. There were harsh lines drawn on her face, wrinkles that showed not just age, but also the hard life she lived. A gaudy purple scarf held back her long gray hair, while large hoop-shaped gold earrings dangled from her ears. It was her dark eyes, though, that I remember most. I feared that if I met her gaze, I might fall into the void of hell itself.

The old woman pulled back one of the curtains around my bed and stared at me. She seemed to look past my face and deep into my soul. After several minutes of this quiet scrutiny, though, she suddenly jumped to her feet and fell backwards, bumping into my mother standing behind her. The Romanian crossed herself and made the sign of the evil eye with trembling hands. "Mon Dieu," she whispered as the color drained from her face.

My mother cursed under her breath, frustrated at this strange behavior. She grabbed the old woman by the shoulders and forcibly turned her around. "What is it, woman! Spit it out!" my mother demanded.

The Romanian swayed back and forth, her mouth opening and closing, saying nothing.

My mother's patience ran out as she tightened her grip and shook the old woman.

The Romanian took a deep breath and uttered a single word, her voice barely above a whisper. "Mullo."

My mother shook the woman again.

The Romanian spoke once more, this time in French. "Vampyr," the crone hissed as she crossed herself three times and tried to break from my mother's grasp.

I listened and observed from where I lay.

My mother growled. "How do I save her? How do I save my daughter?"

Tears formed in the Romanian's frightened eyes. The old woman answered, but her voice shook as she muttered, "Blood, she needs blood."

Something settled upon the room, as if warmth descended upon us with the truth. My mother let go of the woman and smiled.

The Romanian walked away as if to leave, but my mother grabbed her by her long hair and yanked her back.

"Then blood she will have," my mother replied calmly as she pulled a small knife from the bodice of her dress and cut the woman's throat.

The Romanian gurgled as blood poured from the wound. Something awoke in me, strange and sweet, as the coppery scent of blood filled the room. I felt a longing as hunger rose within me. I finally understood all.

My mother shoved the Romanian on the bed, where the old woman landed in a bloody heap on my ivory lace sheets.

"Drink," my mother said.

I licked my lips and did as I was told, suddenly finding an energy I did not know I possessed. I launched myself at the woman and pulled her towards me as if she weighed no more than the sheets upon which I lay. When my mouth found the fount of blood streaming from her neck, I drank.

This is life. This is who I am.

This was my first lesson of many in my education as a vampire. But it was the most important lesson that I ever learned: I needed to drink blood to survive.

Although I was already more mature than most children my age, perhaps because of my early flirting with sickness and death, I still struggled to understand what I was.

My mother, though, seemed prepared to accept this new life and quickly told me that she would become my biggest champion, taking care of those little things that I was still too young to see to myself.

Once my mother discarded of the old woman's body, she called me into the parlor and bade me sit in the worn red velvet chaise that faced opposite of where she stood. She knelt at the foot of the chair, where my legs dangled from its edges, and took my hand. "Cherie, you are not like other children," she said. "You are special. One of a kind. Just like I always knew you were."

The coppery taste of blood was still fresh on my tongue, but I frowned as something lingered in the back of my mind. Even as a child, I understood that killing the Romanian violated one of the first rules of humanity, one of the ten commandments. Drinking the Romanian's blood healed me, but it left me with a lingering guilt.

"We must take this journey together because there is much for us to learn." Mother let go of my hand and delicately touched my plump cheek using her thumb to wipe traces of blood from my bottom lip. "I know little of vampyr ways, but what I know is that you will need to eat. And I promise you, that as your mother, I will never let you go hungry."

I nodded, my thoughts still confused and chaotic. I felt strong and healthy, but I also felt like I had stolen this new vitality, that it was something I did not have the right to possess.

"So here is what we shall do," she explained as she stood. She began to pace the length of the brown rug at her feet. "When you next grow hungry, you will let me know, oui? And I will bring a meal to you, as you wish."

What sort of mother has such a conversation with a child? The answer is a mother with a vampire for a child. My mother was hardly ever conventional and yet I never doubted that she loved me, but everything inside of me was screaming that this was wrong: that *I* was somehow inherently wrong.

"Yes, maman," I answered obediently, as I tried to hide those feelings of guilt, those things that made me human.

The Romanian woman's blood sustained me for over a month before the first hunger pangs arrived. It was as if there was a dragon sleeping within my gut, one that slowly woke up and realized that it needed food, that it needed prey. It started out as a small want, but then it slowly became a pain, and the sickness threatened to take over my body once more.

But my guilt and stubborn nature prevented me from going to my mother as promised and I did my best to hide my decline from her. But I did not understand the hold that my condition held over me, not until it was too late.

I was cooped up in the house as winter raged outside, warming my hands over a fire in the kitchen, as the cook stood nearby and prepared our dinner. The heady scent of rosemary and thyme filled the room. Her son, William, an 8-year-old boy with curly brown hair and chubby cheeks, sat in the corner, watching me. I stared back and suddenly, it was as if all thought and reason left my body. My spirit floated somewhere above me as I walked over to the boy and took him by the hand, asking him if he wanted to play a game with me.

I possessed charms even then, and William could not resist them. He followed me out of the kitchen without a word. I led him into the parlor and instructed him to sit on the floor, which he did without question. I wandered over to the fireplace, beside which sat my mother's sewing basket. I pulled out a small embroidery needle and sat cross-legged in front of the boy, gesturing for him to give me his hand.

He did as I asked.

I grabbed him and stabbed the end of his finger with the needle and quickly brought the finger to my mouth, sucking on it. Droplets of blood slid across my tongue and down my throat, that exquisite elixir of life. I sucked blood from his finger for several minutes and then let go, licking my lips, but still not feeling sated.

Although he was still and compliant, he suddenly seemed to come to his senses and ran from the room.

I was still hungry. And now, it was as if it were worse, as if that one little taste made me crave more. And the hunger was so strong that I still felt as if I were a creature behaving outside of myself. The hunger was the only thing that mattered.

I fell back on the rug and stared up at the ceiling, lying there consumed by this great need. I finally called out for my mother.

She came quickly and panicked when she saw the state I was in. She called for the footman.

"Come quickly!" my mother told him, taking his hand and guiding him over to where I lay.

The footman, concerned, leaned over me.

Mother shoved him to his knees and tossed me the little knife that I soon would know so well.

I caught the utensil and, before the man could protest, I slit his throat and attached my lips to his artery. Blood stained my white dress, and the rug beneath me, but much of the blood flowed into me, bringing me life anew. I sucked him dry, drinking until I was full. The man fainted and then died. Once I extricated myself from him, I threw him to the floor, where he landed with a small thud. I tried to push him away with the tip of my foot, staining my delicate white slipper with red in the process.

Mother shook her head at me. "Reinette, cherie, you are so messy. You should be more tidy about your business."

My senses came back to me as I looked upon the scene with alarm. Guilt, that dreaded instrument of terror, overwhelmed me and I stood up and ran from the room in tears.

As distraught as I was, though, I soon understood that I needed to kill to survive. And from then on, my mother and I became a team working toward my special care. As I grew older, she made sure that I never went hungry. She provided me with a meal every month, providing victims from wherever she could find them. Sometimes, it was an orphan child. Sometimes, it was an aristocrat who my mother did not like. Sometimes, Mother would drug my "victims." Sometimes, she pretended that it was a game. But as they came to me, not a single one of them ever expected to find their deaths at the hand of an innocent girl with long curly blond hair and blue eyes.

I was healthy, but certainly not happy. I felt as if the devil himself possessed me, and I believed that the hunger was a demon living inside of me. This demon consumed me while I fed, but after, the "me" I knew would return to commiserate in guilt. My body thrived, while my soul perished.

I was a monster, but my mother would never allow me to say as much. "You are a lion in the world of mice," she often said. "God created you this way. You are what you are and you should never find shame in that."

Her words did little to appease me.

CHAPTER TWO

A lthough every kill and feeding fed into my remorse, I kept those feelings trapped deep inside of myself, afraid to let my mother see them. She was my mentor and role model, and as is so often the case with daughters, I did not ever wish to disappoint the woman who gave birth to me. So I hid the guilt deep within me, although I often cried in the privacy of my bedroom after each of my feedings. I only cried in secret, though, away from my mother's gaze.

I envied her, though. Her air of detachment was the kind one expects from the strong women of that time, the attitude seen in women that were both powerful and wealthy. I wanted to learn from my *maman* and did my best to mimic that detachment, at least while in her presence. Inside and in private, though, shame darkened my heart.

However, my mother was not a foolish woman. Although she never mentioned it, I was certain that she was aware of my internal struggle. Perhaps this is why she decided that I should travel to Poissy and attend school at an Ursuline convent. After all, the Catholic religion is a forgiving one, and it would perhaps give me a chance to confess my sins - to a degree - and receive absolution after each one. Of course, I understood that I could never confess to murder, but to some lesser act, such as thoughts of violence. And I believe that mother thought that this would help me cope with my strong doubts and self-condemnation.

It was also time to begin my education, and where else better for a girl to learn about the world than in a nunnery? At the time, the nunnery was the only place that a woman could find a good education, so off to Poissy I went, where I learned about religion and the Catholic Church, both things neither my mother nor I ever really cared for. But the nuns still had important subjects to teach me: I also learned about art and soon discovered the masters, finding solace and comfort in the Italian Renaissance.

Mother visited me once a month and we would take a carriage to some nearby village or outpost, where she would seduce some poor man or woman into becoming my next meal.

It was a strange life, but I settled into it, if only from routine. The guilt remained, but it seemed that my education was growing my mind and helping me see beyond the simple act of murder that sustained me.

I grew fond of the convent and its stone walls, its winding stairs and its vast libraries. I often recall its damp air and slight mildew scent with fondness.

I also found comfort in the tutelage of the nuns. One might think that they were backwards and submissive, but the Ursuline convent held some of the first feminists of that age. They taught me about the value and strength of women. That is, possibly, the most important reason my mother chose such a place for my education.

Seasons passed, spring to summer, summer to fall, fall to winter. After a year at the convent, life began to feel almost normal for me. I spent most days with the nuns, but my mother made sure that I spent holidays at home in Paris. This meant Christmas in the City of Lights, and for the first time in my young life, I was healthy and happy enough to enjoy it.

On my ninth birthday, mother surprised me with a carriage ride to the Chateau de Chantilly to meet with a woman she only described as "very important." Mother insisted that this visit could alter the very course of my existence, but I had no idea how.

So we rode to the castle, a large architectural wonder that sat just behind a lush garden surrounded by a small body of water,. The castle's domed and turreted roofs jutted menacingly into the gray sky of winter. At the door, we were greeted by a servant who showed us into a large drawing room highlighted with large tapestries depicting stories from ancient Greek mythology. The servant urged us to sit at a small table surrounded by velvet chairs. I took the chair closest to the room's large ornate white marble fireplace. From beyond the room, I could barely make out the sounds of music: someone was singing an aria from *Cadmus et Hermione.*

"Madame de Lebon will be with you shortly," the servant announced before bowing and taking his leave.

I recognized the name because Mother had mentioned her often. Madame de Lebon was a famous fortune teller, known for her accurate predictions for the French nobility and even the royal family. Rumors suggested that King Louis XV himself often consulted her for advice. Many even credited the soothsayer for solving many of France's problems, although historians would argue that the influence of Cardinal Fleury over the King was far more important in bringing France out of its economic and financial woes. Regardless of what the French believed, though, Madame de Lebon held a stellar reputation among those who were most important to French society.

As we sat, I strained my ears to catch more of the opera I heard earlier, but all was suddenly and eerily quiet inside the chateau.

After sitting for an hour, I grew impatient. I wanted to get up and explore the castle grounds, but Mother insisted that I stay put and remain quiet, as little girls must. And like daughters who both admire and fear their mothers, I obeyed. But I was anxious about this meeting, although I hardly understood why.

Eventually, Madame de Lebon presented herself. She was not like what I expected. I thought she might look like my first victim, the old Romanian woman. Instead, Madame de Lebon was an exotic dark-skinned goddess with vibrant black-lined green eyes. Her clothing was unlike anything I had ever seen, embroidered silks in red and gold that seemed to shimmer when she glided into the room. She walked with the air of someone not born on Earth, but a spiritual being come to temporarily visit with mortals.

I sat up straighter in my chair, hoping that this wonderfully interesting woman would notice me.

She approached the table and sat down, every movement seamless and somehow magical. Her eyes fixed on me and she took my hand, speaking, her voice lilting with an accent I did not recognize. "Oh, child, you are as lovely as I've heard," she said.

The scent of tropical spices, heady and strong, overwhelmed me, as her perfume wafted across the table.

My mother preened in her chair. "Isn't she?" she remarked.

I soon realized that this was a preordained meeting, not just by my mother, but perhaps by fate herself.

My mother leaned forward, as much as her tight corset would allow, and addressed the other woman. "So, please, Madame de Lebon, tell me what do you see?"

The fortune teller turned my hand over and stared at my palm. She traced the lines there with her fingers and then looked up to study my face. I flushed at her scrutiny, feeling as if she were gazing deep inside me, learning my secrets and seeing my past, present and future. But if she found alarm in anything she found there, she did not acknowledge it. Instead, she offered a wide smile, her white teeth gleaming at me. She reached up and tapped my nose with her long black finger. "You are everything I thought you would be."

I tilted my head curiously at this enigma of a woman. Although I often thought my mother's belief in the supernatural slightly foolish, I knew I would believe anything Madame de Lebon told me.

The soothsayer dropped my hand and turned her attention to my mother, her voice dropping, becoming more solemn. "Your daughter will become the mistress to King Louis, mark my words," she announced, one delicate hand gesturing at me gracefully.

My mother's eyes widened as she sucked in a deep breath.

My own breath stopped in my throat, and I held it there, realizing that this was one of those moments that would define my entire life.

"I knew it," my mother whispered, bringing her clasped hands to her heart, tears dancing in her eyes. "I knew it the day she was born." She looked at me. "Reinette, *cherie*, you are destined for greatness. Have I not always said that?"

I nodded, dumbfounded.

Mother continued speaking. "Now thank the good Madame for taking this time for us. She is a very busy woman and went out of her way to meet you."

My childish lips felt heavy, but I did as asked. "Thank you," I said.

Both women stood up. My mother clasped the fortune teller's hand, bringing it to her lips graciously. "Thank you so much, Madame. You have truly warmed my heart. I will take the necessary action for Reinette's to find her destined path immediately."

I had no idea what that meant.

Madame de Lebon nodded and looked at me once again, her face warm and friendly. She offered a curt nod before turning around, her silks whisking around behind her as she walked away, disappearing into the next room.

My mother took my hand and pulled me to my feet. "Well, that's done," she remarked. "Now we must make our preparations. Your education must start immediately."

I looked around the room, which suddenly felt cold and barren now that Madame de Lebon was gone from it. "Aren't we staying?" I asked.

Mother shook her head. "Now, we must go home. To Paris. There is much to do and so very little time to do it. Fate has plans for you, *mon cherie*, and I will not let anything stand in its way."

At nine years old, I did not understand the consequences of this encounter and what it meant.. But I still squeezed my mother's hand, entrusting my life and my destiny to her. But I knew that life would change again for me, and that I wouldn't return to the convent. My life as a child was officially over.

Mother and I braved that same cold wintry evening to make the long trip back to Paris. I feigned sleep during the ride to avoid conversation as I tried to wrap my thoughts around what had just happened. I ran over the evening and its conversation in my head and then wondered about what this new education of mine might entail. I already missed the convent and the things the nuns had taught me, but I was also hopeful about what new things I would soon learn and who would serve as my new teachers.

As I was only a girl, I did not understand what it meant, this becoming mistress to a king. I was too young to understand affairs of a sexual nature, but I did know that such an appointment was a prestigious one. I also understood that it would involve living at court, surrounded by many of the things I already loved: architecture, paintings, beautiful clothes and intelligent conversation.

Eventually, my mind wore itself out and I fell asleep. I do not remember anyone carrying me up to my bedchamber that evening and undressing me and putting me to bed, but I woke the next morning with sunshine streaming through my window, frost clinging to the glass. There was knocking at the door, a maid pleading with me to quickly get dressed and come downstairs immediately.

My new life had already begun. I quickly chose my favorite dress, a concoction of blue ruffles and lace, and had the maid help me put it on. I slid a pair of delicate blue jeweled slippers on my feet as the maid fussed with my long hair, adjusting it in a way that would flatter my perfect porcelain face. She quickly explained that I would soon meet my new tutors and begin going over a plan for my education. They were to evaluate my reading, math, art appreciation and other skills to determine where to begin.

Once dressed, I hurried downstairs, the maid fretting over me. I found my mother in the parlor, entertaining our visitors. The room was full of laughter and conversation. A large fire burned in the fireplace, warming the chill air of winter. Embers floated around it in a haze, seemingly caught up with the chaos seeking to organize itself in that room.

As I walked into the room, our visitors organized themselves into a perfect line. These were my tutors, those people who would help shape the next five years of my life.

Mother hurried to my side and took my hand, taking me down the line, introducing each teacher to me. I offered them a small curtsy, for these were no ordinary men and women. These were acclaimed professors, dancers, singers and art historians. They were the cream of educated society and I could only imagine how much time and money my mother spent in gathering them at our house in such a quick and efficient manner. I was most excited to meet Pierre Jelyotte, one of the greatest opera singers of our time, who bowed to me, just a child, and told me that he looked forward to working with me.

At the time, I had no idea where the money came from to pay such tutelage, but I later learned that mother worked out a financial arrangement with my legal guardian, Le Normant de Tourneham. As I previously wrote, it was likely that de Tourneham was my father, especially as he took a special interest in me, although I rarely saw him in person. His money, though, was always around us, and I now believe that he paid for most of my childhood luxuries, as well as for my education.

Once introduced to my new tutors, I took time with each to answer questions about things children love to speak of: hopes, dreams and passions.

And so my life as a young adult began, all at the tender age of nine. The next few years of my life were nothing but lessons, all priming me to achieve the destiny laid out for me by Madame de Lebon.

CHAPTER THREE

My life became a series of lessons that covered a variety of subjects, including philosophy, mathematics, literature and science. I could easily hold discussions with adults twice my age, and as I became more sheltered from other children, I often preferred the company of my elders. I was a young woman in the making, a woman ahead of her time and exactly who my mother wanted me to be.

As I grew into my teens, I began to take delight in the arts, particularly singing, dancing and acting. Although my first performances were for the benefit of my mother, tutors and household staff, I eventually gained the opportunity to spread my wings and perform in public. I was a common sight at the notorious Club de L'Entresol, a think tank group that met every Saturday at the home of the great historian, Charles Jean-Francois Heanult. Although the club was gentlemen-only, it occasionally allowed women into its top secret meetings for entertainment. The club invited me often to perform Shakespearean monologues or sing songs about our French heritage. The men also delighted in conversing with a young well-educated woman.

Eventually, one of the club regulars approached me about performing in a production of Romeo & Juliet, a play I was already very familiar with. Its story appealed to my teen sensibilities: two doomed lovers. Little did I know that play would serve as an outline for my teenage life.

I gained the role of Juliet in a production by one of the best acting troupes of our time, Le Mystere. The troupe's reputation preceded it all over France and they even had experience in performing for the King.

At first, Mother balked at the idea, thinking it was a waste, but I explained that it would increase my influence with the Club, as well as the noble gentlemen who were members. I eventually wore her down and she agreed to let me begin attending rehearsals. I was delighted.

It was during my first rehearsals when the group took me on as one of their own.

But it was one actor, specifically, that garnered my attention. His name was Phillipe, and he was the Romeo to my Juliet.

We were well cast: me, the beautiful ingenue destined for greatness, and he, the talented orphan boy taken in by an acting troupe.

I loved Phillipe from the moment I first saw him: the scruffy French boy with the dark curly locks that fell into deep and passionate blue eyes. There was an air of danger to him, probably because of his birth, that appealed to my sense of teenage rebellion. I had never wanted anything more for myself than this boy.

It soon became evident that Phillipe felt the same. Although the troupe praised us both for our acting, our scenes together were real and heartfelt. We were the shining example of Shakespeare's words: two lovers torn apart by their familial backgrounds.

But a rose is a rose by any other name, is it not?

We pretended that our passions were all for show. But then it came time to practice the balcony scene, which would end with a kiss.

"Oh, Romeo, Romeo," my wistful Juliet spoke from a balcony made of thick poles and thin boards. "Wherefore art thou, Romeo?" I called out to my beloved, both in character and as Reinette.

When Phillipe appeared on stage just below me, time slowed to a halt. I felt my pulse pounding in my ears, my cheeks flushed and my stomach filled with butterflies. A swell of emotions washed over me.

Phillipe spoke his lines, one hand pressed against his chest. "I take thee at thy word: call me but love, and I'll be new baptized; Henceforth, I never will be Romeo."

He climbed the small metal railing that led up to where I stood and then took my hand.

A fire burned within me, unlike anything I had ever felt before.

He pressed a hand against my cheek and pulled me closer until our lips touched in the kiss that would seal the doomed couple's fate. Phillipe smelled of sawdust and musk, masculine and heady. I drowned in his scent and his kiss. The world fell away.

I felt faint, outside of myself, floating around just above the stage.

Surely, this was love. This is what it felt like.

Monsieur Delacourte, the director, cleared his throat loudly. The world fell back into place as we pulled away from each other. But I still felt as if I were drifting above the stage, trapped in that kiss.

The expression on Monsieur Delacourte's face, though, brought me back to reality. He seemed concerned. I quickly disentangled myself from Phillipe's embrace and climbed down the stairs behind the fake balcony, using my considerable acting skills to express disinterest, channeling my mother.

"Are we done for the day?" I asked, almost as if put out, as I approached the front of the stage. "I have a dinner that I simply cannot miss."

I could feel Phillipe's confusion as he watched me walk away, but Monsieur Delacourte sighed in relief and waved me away with a hand, smiling.

I was a such good little actress. But my face was still warm and my breath still heavy during the carriage ride home, in spite of the chilly autumn wind blowing in from the north that stirred up not just leaves, but passions.

We rehearsed that scene dozens of times and yet it never lost its potency. My affair with Philipe also spread offstage: he and I began to meet and embrace in private. I was in love and it was exhilarating.

But love, especially the first, is also careless. We were young and stupid, certain that we would never get caught, that no one could tell that we had feelings for each other. Teens rarely feel that the world touches them, and it was our certainty of our invincibility that was our undoing.

We were not invulnerable to fate, that all-powerful device that held my life dangling over a never-ending abyss. Had I forgotten my place? Had I forgotten that I would save myself to become mistress to a King? Did I not know that the spinster that we called fate would never allow me to become the lover or the wife of a poor actor?

Our secret seemed safe, at least until the night of our performance. The club invited the public to attend. This included my mother, who seemed to have an eye for deceit. Although she praised my performance after the play, she grabbed my hand and pulled me away from the club. Once we were outside and away from the crowd, she began scolding me.

"Your days as an actress are over," she said, hissing the words between her teeth. "You are to never step foot in this club again. You have more important things to attend to."

Although she had not said it, I knew she had seen through my deception and understood the nature of my relationship with my co-star. Phillipe and I thought we were so careful, and yet, Mother knew. She probably knew well before our performance, and only allowed us to finish the show, for propriety's sake. She would not want the noblemen of the club to think of me as anything but pure and chaste. God forbid that news spread all over Paris that I was anything but before destiny put me in the King's court.

After escorting me home, Mother locked me in my room. For several weeks, I was only allowed access to our house, with strict rules that I would not step outside our front door. Mother was as cruel a mistress as fate. She was also more clever than I gave her credit for because when my monthly feeding time came, she remembered my indiscretions.

Some things we never forget, including those moments when we must choose the path our lives take.

As a punishment, Mother made me wait three days after my usual feeding time, so that when she turned up with the victim, I was dazed by hunger, more animal than human. Perhaps that's why I did not pay it any mind when she finally shoved a tall man into the room. A cloth bag covered his head and a thick rope bound his hands together.

I lunged for him and then stopped myself. In spite of the hunger, I suddenly felt ill.

My mother swung her cane and hit the man behind his knees, forcing him to bow in front of me. After she pulled the bag away from his head, his dark hair fell softly around his face.

I stared at Philipe as the hunger gnawed away inside me.

"No," I whispered, taking a step back, shaking my head in abject horror.

But that thing inside of me, that thing that wanted blood, kept rising, making me feel like I might burn up from the inside out.

"Take care of this once and for all, Reinette," my mother demanded from where she stood, behind Phillipe, her arms crossed in front of her. She did not raise her voice, but remained detached, composed, as was her way.

I had a choice, and I quickly imagined grabbing Philippe and running out of there, running away from her and this life that held me captive.

But my mother was also inside my head and asked if I, a future mistress to a king, could ever become a lowly actor's wife? If I could make due with roaming from village to village, performing for dollars? It was certainly a glamorous idea to my teenager's mind, but the pragmatist part of myself knew better.

As reality dawned on me, I stared at my mother, my jaw slack.

And I was so very hungry.

I licked my lips as I thought of my future life, the one destiny held for me. I imagined myself at the side of the King, his mistress, a woman of high esteem, dancing in beautiful rooms built of wood and glass, my body covered in expensive fabrics, furs and diamond-laden jewelry.

The pragmatist in my head told me that if I continued to behave like a love-sick child, I would never have that. That life would disappear.

I was only 15 years old, but on that day, I became a woman.

Philippe's eyes remained closed in fear.

"Look at me," I said, my voice trembling.

He did as asked and saw me standing there. "My sweet Reinette," he cried, tears slipping down his cheeks. "My sweet beautiful Reinette."

I knew that if I did not act quickly, I would remain rooted in my indecision forever.

And I was so very hungry.

I fell upon him quickly. I pulled my knife from my bodice and slit his throat before he could utter another word. My mouth found his neck before I could watch his face go slack, before I could see his eyes roll up into the back of his head. I drank and drank, never seeming to get my fill. Philipe's life poured out of his body and into me.

Eventually, I shoved him away, his blood working through my system and into my heart, where he would always live as a part of me.

Mother quickly removed the limp body from my presence, perhaps understanding my lingering feelings for the boy, my first real love.

I slumped to the floor, my head pressed against its wooden slats, mourning for everything that I had lost. I was not aware that I was capable of so many tears, yet they stained the wood beneath me, gathering into a pool of my grief.

Seconds became minutes, minutes became hours, but eventually my tears began to dry. I lifted my head and stood up, staring at the portrait that hung over my bed. It was a painting of me at ten years old, done to celebrate my "miraculous recovery" from my long illness. Now, the portrait only represented something gone, innocence lost.

In my short time standing there, I learned to hate that portrait. I lashed at it, jumping on my bed and attacking the canvas with my bloody little knife. I slashed at my child's face and its bright eyes gleaming back at me, knowing that I would never know such joy again. That child no longer existed, so I destroyed her likeness with my knife and my anger. I slashed until the canvas became shreds and then pulled the wooden frame from the wall and threw it against the floor where it broke into several pieces.

A calm came over me, the such I had never known. I felt emotion begin to flit away from me, like so many butterflies on a windy day.

I was a woman and I put away childish things. Little Reinette was dead. Long live Madame de Pompadour.

CHAPTER FOUR

Ipushed all emotion, sadness and guilt down into the deepest part of my heart and rededicated my time to my education. I began to learn from my tutors and my mother. I received lessons on the "important" things, like how to fit into proper society. But I also learned how to place a careful shield around my heart, protecting it from any further breakage. I was still charming, as well as beautiful, but I also learned to become aloof.

This new ice around my heart, as well as my beauty, became my greatest strength. Although my education made me a well-rounded individual, it was these other two assets that had suitors throwing themselves at my feet.

Mother, though, discouraged any and all potential husbands. I was destined for greater things. But fate often throws wrenches into well-made plans and, sometimes, even destiny itself must choose a path on a forked road.

Mother and I celebrated my 19th birthday in our usual fashion: out on the town, dining at a fine salon. But the usual soon turned into a whirling dervish.

Inebriated on food and wine, we rode home in our carriage as the rest of that night fell around us, the lights of candles and lamps tucked away in windows the only illumination we saw. As our horses carried our vehicle through the streets of Paris, Mother turned to me and took my hand. Her lavender perfume filled the carriage as she looked down, refusing to meet my gaze. "Reinette, I have something to confess."

I stared at her, blinking, my body fatigued from the evening's merriment. I preferred to rest on the way home, but Mother, and fate, had other ideas. "What is it?" I asked and then yawned, lifting a delicate hand to cover my mouth.

"Our money… it is…" Mother hesitated and placed a hand on her ample breast. "It is gone. We are destitute. Poor. We have nothing."

I raised an eyebrow as understanding slowly came to me. However, I nearly accused her of joking, that is until I saw the tears in her eyes. Although she had as much a talent for the dramatic as I, there was truth in her expression.

"But how? Why?" I asked, feeling as if the carriage had hit a large pothole and was now bouncing upwards towards the sky.

My mother shook her head, "It doesn't matter."

I opened my mouth to protest, but closed it again. I had so many questions, but I knew this had something to do with what I perceived as a falling out with our benefactor, my legal guardian, Le Normant de Tournehem.

"I have a plan," my mother continued.

I nodded, silent, as dread began to push through the cage around my heart. I swallowed all emotion, though, and maintained a blank expression. When I spoke, my voice was calm. "And my destiny? The King?" I merely asked, as if I were inquiring about the time we were meant to have dinner.

This was something I then realized that was more important to me than I ever knew. I had given up so much of myself for the destiny given to me by a fortuneteller.

"You are to marry Charles," she said, still keeping her eyes averted.

I did not understand. I played Madame de Lebon's words over and over in my mind. My fate was supposedly clear, was it not? "Charles?" I asked. "You mean Le Normant's nephew?" Suddenly, things began to make sense. Of course, my guardian would have designs of his own. And as a woman, my fate was never tied up with what I wanted, but with what men in power over me intended. "But what about my destiny? What about the king?" I asked again. I knew then that going to court and becoming a mistress was far better than becoming the wife of a simple noble.

Mother finally lifted her head to look at me, a calculated expression painted on her face as clearly as the rouge dotted on her cheeks. "I know it may not make sense, dear daughter, but I feel that this is the path you need to take. For now. But you will become the woman you must become."

I shook my head, loose blond curls bouncing around my face. "But what about the king?" I asked for the third time.

Mother inhaled and answered. "Charles is well-connected. And in this, Le Normant insists. This position comes with enough money to save us from poverty."

I stared at her, as if she spoke a language I did not comprehend.

She continued, "He is also the sole heir to Le Normant's estate. He will take you the places you need to go, including court."

Suddenly, it dawned on me. My mother would not give up our chances at court so easily. This was not some ill-conceived plot to pull me from my destiny. Mother was using this to get me to the King.

Mother was not a fool. Even at 19, I knew this. And so I would do what she said. Because, more than likely, she was right.

We spent the rest of the ride home in silence. I gazed out the small window of the city I loved, a place which held such hope and promise for me, but also much defeat. I began to understand what it meant to exist as a woman in a world that believed that women only existed for men. My life was always decided by men, but it did not change my goals and aims. I would marry Charles and, perhaps, I would make a good wife. Maybe I would even give him children, although something told me that was impossible due to my nature. I could pretend happiness, but all the while keep my dignity and wait for the opportunity to strike.

This was my duty now, as a woman, as my mother's daughter.

But I would do more, too, and I knew it. Because as mother pointed out, Charles *was* well-connected. And I would use my beauty and my charms not to just woo him, but to woo all the people of high society around him. I would woo my way through him to the King.

I would not give up my dream so easily.

And so, at the age of 19, I married Charles Guillaume Le Normant d'Etiolles. My wedding day is still something of a blur, an event where I just went through the motions. I vaguely recall wearing a dress chosen for me by my mother, but I barely remember uttering those empty vows about obeisance and honor. The wedding was a means to an end: to secure finances for our family and to use my new position as a way to get to the King. I bedded my husband, on our wedding night, not out of passion, but duty.

Ironically, my new husband adored me greatly, even in spite of my cold demeanor towards him and my usual blank attitude. He moved us to the estate of Etiolles, a very large manor on a massive piece of property that contained its own hunting grounds. I insisted that mother come with us, though, stressing that I could not leave her behind in Paris to waste away without her beloved daughter and best friend. This was, of course, all a part of the plan, something Mother and I discussed before the nuptials.

Charles agreed because he was very much in love with me.

My relationship with my mother continued as always: she helped me find victims and I fed in secrecy, safe from the prying eyes of everyone else in our lives. No one ever need know what I was.

My life was not my own, but I was biding my time.

I gave Charles two children, although they were not actually mine. But Charles loved me so much that he believed me when I told him that I needed to escape to warmer climes for my faked pregnancies, leaving him to continue his own work so that I could go somewhere warm, where mother and I arranged to secretly adopt infants from orphanages. Unfortunately, both orphans were sickly, the first not even making it to the age of one. The other only had 10 years in this world. I always imagined this was fate's way of telling me that being a wife and mother was not for me.

I felt nothing for those children or my husband. But I lived on, my heart still trapped in a cage of my making.

Mother hired painters to do elaborate portraits of me, and

we gifted these works of art not to family, but to those in and around the French court. Mother planned on making my face one of the most well known in all the country, and in that, she succeeded: word of my beauty spread all over Paris and beyond. Meanwhile, Charles took me to grand balls and elite gatherings that included some of the highest-ranking nobles in the city.. We also hosted our own lavish events at Etiolles. I even founded my own salon there and it included some of the best minds in the world, such as Voltaire. The reputation of my intelligence and beauty became known throughout France. I held a very public life and moved in every circle I found, all with one goal in mind: to get to the king.

Eventually, everything fell into place, according to plan. The minor setback of my marriage was only a stepping stone on my path to meet my destiny.

While the king mourned the loss of his third mistress, the duchesse de Chateauroux, my mother and I moved through social circles that took advantage of that loss and promoted me to His Highness. He received my portraits, along with word of my charm, beauty and intellect.

I soon received an official invitation to visit the Palace of Versailles for a masked ball to celebrate the marriage of the Dauphin of France. The invitation came from the King himself, who would also attend the grand event.

Fate called me like never before.

Mother and I fretted over dresses for the ball and went through many dressmakers before finding one that could meet the vision we wanted for my gown. The result was a dark blue ball gown with tiny silver star-shaped beads sewn throughout its lace. The dressmaker worked long hours to assure that it fit, and it was perfect: its color accented my eyes and highlighted my porcelain skin. Its shape showed off my symmetrically oval face and the rounding curves of my body.

My entrance to the ball was also well-thought out, and although I left Paris early on that evening, we took the trip at a leisurely pace. The evening was so cold that I used furs to cover up as I rode. But the plan was that I would arrive just ever so slightly late, because a true Frenchwoman never arrived on time. This was my grand entrance into the court of royalty. Perfection was key.

This was my night and I would reign as the star of the ball.

At Versailles, I shrugged out of my furs before stepping out of the carriage, my bare arms only draped with a stole. I was cold, but acted otherwise, as if there was some ethereal heat burning deep within my breast. I made my way into the palace proper. Servants instructed me to wait just behind a set of double doors as someone on the other side announced my presence. After the doors opened, I glided into the ballroom and stood at the top of a small staircase. All eyes turned to me. I flushed, using the most of my acting skills to pretend that I was not used to such attention, although I certainly was. I held my head high as I took in the measure of the room.

Everything was gold. There were gold fixtures on the ceiling and gold candles flickered from chandeliers. Pink and blue walls held ornate gold carvings and there were portraits hanging on them in golden frames. Although the night outside was dark, the massive room was aglow with light and laughter, of people enjoying themselves.

I confidently strode into the room, as an orchestra began a waltz. A moustached man with curly brown hair that touched his shoulders bowed to me and asked me to dance. I took his hand and deftly followed him, swinging quickly into the movements that I was all too familiar with. It did not matter who this man was. The only thing that mattered was the impression that I made as I flowed around the room in his embrace. I was the brightest light in that room, even brighter than the candles hanging above us. And as I dance, my gaze found King Louis XV sitting in a chair at the head of the room, carefully watching me, smiling.

Something stirred within me, something akin to feelings, and I allowed myself this brief glimpse of joy. I felt butterflies in my stomach as the King continued to study me, even as I accepted the next dance invitation and the next, knowing that I had his full and undivided attention.

I turned down my fourth dance invitation to join a small

group of men and women that I knew from my salon. But I felt Louis' eyes following me as I crossed the room: they burned through the back of my dress as I stood with my friends, who were discussing such delicate matters as fashion, roses and porcelain.

The conversation was only my means to an end, though, because soon, one of the King's men approached me.

"Madame," the man said as he gave me a terse bow.

I turned around to acknowledge him, all of my movements carefully plotted.

"Could you come with me, Madame?" he asked and offered his arm.

"Bien sur," I replied as I placed a gloved hand on his elbow. I knew where he would take me.

We walked across the room together, arm in arm, to where the King sat on his royal throne. I finally allowed myself to take the time to admire the man behind the title, noting that he was a handsome fellow, something I had not expected. Like most royalty, his features were delicate and nearly feminine, although his nose turned up in a very masculine manner. A blue silk ribbon tied back his long dark wavy hair and dimples showed in his cheeks when he smiled, something he did quite often. He seemed benevolent, but powerful, oozing a charm that was equal to my own. As he stood there confidently, regarding me in the same way, I knew that we were a good match.

I smiled, but not because it was part of the act, but because I allowed some small amount of happiness to seep into my protected heart. My dull life as a wife and mother was now over: this man would take me away from all that.

I curtsied, as one must, but when I looked up, Louis was standing directly in front of me. He took my hand and helped me to stand up again.

"That won't be necessary, Madame," he said.

I allowed my gaze to meet his, a bold move, but I did not fear what he might do to me. In that moment, everything became simple as my life fell back into place.

CHAPTER FIVE

After the ball, I stayed on as a guest at Versailles with Louis often at my side. In just a month, he had me moved into an apartment directly above his royal chambers. Although I had already waited many long years for my status as King's mistress to finally happen, it still felt as if my achievement occurred overnight.

The carriage had not only left the station but now rolled down the mountain in a desperate chase to get to its destination in record time.

As expected, my mother helped me in all things, even in arranging for an attorney to end my marriage to Charles quickly. I no longer had need for a doting husband, for I was a ward of the King. I moved forward without ever looking back, as was my way. I denied Charles a proper goodbye, and I only raised an eyebrow when receiving reports that our separation devastated him.

There was no guilt, though, in my deception, because in spite of the fluttery feelings deep within my belly that began when I met King Louis, I still had my heart carefully trapped behind icy walls. Now, I was no one's wife, although I was someone's mistress, but that new position offered me a freedom that many women of my standing rarely had. France was now laid out before me as if it were a feast, every dish mine for the taking.

I fed on blood, thanks to my mother and a group of faithful servants that she paid to never ask questions. Mother grew more careful in choosing my victims, though, because now all eyes of the world were on me. So I went from dining on nobility to drinking from the homeless, the orphans and the downtrodden, those outcast people that no one would ever miss. I still believe that I gave them a fate, death, that was far better than the barren existence they might find on their own.

My life was good and my time with Louis proved enjoyable. I did not have to worry about love because mistresses were not meant for such foolish notions. There was no pressure for me to act as if I were a wife because I was not one. However, I enjoyed spending time with the king, as we quickly realized that we shared the same interests in things that mattered: art, music and architecture. We laughed at the same jokes. We found delight not just in each others' bodies, but with each others company, too.

I was finally free of the womanly chains that bound most of my life. I daresay I was almost happy.

I did not become official mistress, though, until later. Even after the King offered me the title of Marquise of the estate of Pompadour, there were some nobles who thought I was ill-suited to serve the court in any official capacity. But I had many friends at Versailles, including the Princess de Conti, the King's cousin, who officially introduced me to court in September of that same year.

Court etiquette came easily to me and, eventually, I managed to win over many of my detractors. By December, I was well on my way to having the respect of an entire nation.

Fate, though, is a cruel mistress, and sometimes she often likes to throw thorns into the plans of those she controls. My first holiday season at Versailles brought grief as my mother fell seriously ill.

Although I spent most of Christmas morning tending to my mother, who seemed closer to recovery at the time, I spent the rest of my afternoon preparing for an evening with the king. It was court tradition that the king spent days with his wife, but his nights belonged to me, even on holidays.

Two of my attendants helped me get dressed in a beautiful dark green gown made of velvet and lace, while another placed an ostentatious diamond necklace around my neck, one of many expensive gifts from Louis.

So I assumed that when there was a knock on the door, it was the king summoning me. "Enter," I announced as my attendants put the finishing touches in my hair, pinning it up with delicate diamond clasps and pulling curls down to frame my petite face and across my swan-like neck.

A man came through the door and bowed, but I recognized him as one of my mother's servants, not someone from the King. His face was grim and his eyes told all.

I curled my hand into a fist and clenched it against my breast, fearing the worse.

"Madame," he said, doing everything he could from meeting my gaze.

I offered a slight nod of my head to encourage him to continue.

"It's your mother," he stated, shaking his head back and forth.

Despair fell around me, the tone of his voice unmistakable. I knew what he would say before he said it. "She's dead," I announced to the room, as tears formed in my eyes.

"Yes, madame," the servant admitted, still averting his eyes, looking at everything in the room but me.

As all air seemed to leave the room, Louis burst into my apartments, still in his stockinged feet, his jacket askew and his hair messy. He ran to my side and took both of my hands in his. "Reinette, my darling, I heard, I am so sorry."

I fell into his embrace, my knees buckling underneath me. Although I had known death my entire life, it had never felt so personal. Perhaps it was because this was a death that I could not control. Mother was gone and if there was any innocence remaining within me, it fled with her passing.

I clung to Louis and wept not just for my mother, but for that childhood now irretrievably lost. All those emotions I bottled up streamed out of me at once, and I thought I might drown in the tears they left in their wake.

Mother would never see my official recognition as the King's mistress, something as important to her as it was to me. As I lay in my lover's arms, I swore that I would not only gain that title, but serve in that position for her and in honor of her. It was my last duty as a daughter, the last piece of myself that I had to give.

I have no idea how long I found solace in Louis' arms, but the sobs gradually became quiet tears and, eventually, I extricated myself from his embrace.

Louis stared down at me, bringing his hands up to cup my cheeks, using the back of his thumb to wipe traces of my tears away.

I closed my eyes and inhaled, taking in the room's scents and sounds. There was some sniffling from the servants, in grief. I smelled fresh lavender just brought into my room earlier in that day from the palace gardens. I centered myself on the moment and thought only of myself being rooted to that place. I felt my feet struggling to breathe in shoes that were about a half size too small and I felt the corset around me constricting my waist. I focused completely on my senses, letting the emotions begin to drift away.

"Thank you," I whispered to Louis, once I knew my voice would not tremble or betray me.

I looked around the room, realizing that other servants were surrounding us, some holding trays of meats, cheeses and boxes wrapped in colorful fabrics. Louis nodded to one of them and they began setting up tables with their treats around the room. Louis had still brought Christmas to me in my grief.

Perhaps I should have loved him for doing that, and perhaps I did, if only because he was my King. But the walls around my heart only allowed so much feeling into them before they shut down again. I had expended most of that on mourning for my mother.

And so, mother went into the earth. Another year came and went. As time passed, I finally began to find the recognition that I deserved. I still had my enemies, including women who sought to replace me, but I was clever and made arrangements to marry them off to nobles before they ever had a chance to threaten my position. I understood that my new place of prominence was a precarious one, something I would often have to fight for. But it also meant that I needed to ally myself with powerful people, which I continued to do.

One of those people was the Queen, the King's wife. And although one might think that a King's mistress and his Queen would find themselves at odds, I still made a show of requesting a special audience with Her Majesty, something no other mistress had ever done before.

Perhaps I was wise beyond my years, or perhaps my mother had taught me well.

Although the Queen quietly acknowledged my presence when we attended the same events, it wasn't until our first formal meeting that our alliance began. I was not certain she would even agree to meet with me, but she did. That surprised us both.

Going into that meeting, I put all my prejudices and thoughts aside. I was merely a woman fulfilling her duty to her King. One of the Queen's maids in waiting came to fetch me at the appointed time and proceeded to lead me through the many golden halls of Versailles. I followed the servant obediently with my usual charm and grace, but without any pretense. As we stopped in front of the Queen's meeting rooms, the maid motioned for me to go through a large set of engraved doors at the end of a long hallway.

I pushed against the doors, which gave, allowing me to step into the room. The smell of lilacs filled the air, an odor coming from the several large vases placed around the room, all filled with flowers. The room, though, was hot and stuffy, the result of a particularly humid summer day. I felt sweat sticking to the back of my neck as tendrils of my hair began to loosen themselves from my carefully styled coif.

The Queen sat at the far end of the room, waving a jewel-encrusted fan in front of her face. I took several more steps into the room and curtsied, and waited for further instructions.

"There, there," the Queen said. "There's no need for that." She fluttered her free hand at the two servants standing behind her, dismissing them from their duties.

As the servants scurried off through a back door, the Queen stood up and quietly placed her fan in her now-empty chair.

She approached me and took my hand.

This is the first time that I was close enough to Her Majesty to allow myself to study her appearance. She was a beautiful woman, although the aging process had begun, hinting that her beauty would soon begin to fade. But I saw something in her deep green eyes that I admired, a strength and intelligence that I often recognized within myself.

"I believe we should become friends, Your Majesty," I simply stated, having rehearsed those words so many times inside my head. It was presumptive, but I thought I knew exactly what I was doing.

The Queen smiled and nodded in agreement. "Call me Marie. I harbor no ill will towards you, Reinette. I do so hope you realize that, as my husband's mistress. I actually see you as my equal. We both care for the same man, true, but we are also both noble and intellectual women. Let's do what is best for the King and for France. So yes, let us become good friends."

I nodded and smiled. This had gone better than I had anticipated. "Your wish is my command, Marie," I answered.

Marie fanned herself with her hand, "It's so hot in here. Come, let's go for a walk outside," She dropped my hand and then offered her arm instead.

I looped my arm around hers as we exited the meeting room by a side door that led into the grand gardens. The scent of roses surrounded us as we began to discuss all the things we loved, all those things we had in common: books, art, literature, philosophy and even the King. This was the beginning of our great friendship.

When I wasn't spending time in the company of Louis or Marie, I was busy making alliances at court. When a diplomat of Austria begged for my assistance with the Treaty of Versailles, I played an important part in making sure that Louis signed it. This treaty allied France with Austria, a country formerly considered one of our enemies. But thanks to me, Austria became a friend. That meant when Britain and Prussia came to our shores to attack France, we went to war with our allies to protect what was ours.

That war, though, did not go as planned. Not only did we suffer terrible losses, but the cost of battle bankrupted and diminished France's place in the world.

Do I have regrets? No. To this day, I maintain that I held the right decision in encouraging France to become allies with Austria. And although we did not win the war, we did not lose our country to Britain or Prussia who had plans to seize France and make her their own. Although we lost our dignity, we did not lose ourselves.

Louis was heartbroken, though, over the turn of events after the war. This led to him spending many evenings suffering from new anxieties. He called for me nearly every night after the war, bringing me into his bedchamber to sing him to sleep, to enchant him with lovely songs about better times and the superiority of France.

As the King's fears got the better of him, I supported some of France's most important economic ministers and financial advisors. And because of this, France recovered, although she was no longer considered the great power of Europe. That honor now belonged to Britain. But France rallied once more and stood proud.

However, my enemies increased in number. They blamed me for the downfall of the country. They called me less than desirable names in public and even worse names in private. They drew up pamphlets denouncing me and the power they thought I held over the King.

My relationship with the King and Queen, though, protected me. The people could complain all they want, but my position at Court was always safe.

Eventually, the country recovered, but Louis continued to slip into great bouts of depression. The Queen and I grew to worrying more about him. We spent much time together planning great events and celebrations, anything entertaining that we could think of, to keep the King happy.

Louis appreciated our efforts and sometimes rewarded us with a smile, but he would then return to the pit of despair that threatened to drown him. His low moods increased with each passing day. And the people began to talk: they feared that the mind of the King was lost.

I grew weary of being held responsible for his state of mind and felt suffocated by the burden of my responsibility in keeping the King's spirits up. Because of this, I knew that my time at Versailles would eventually need to end, particularly since the King's many moods also affected my ability to woo and seduce him. He began to call for me less, sequestering himself in his chambers away from the world that made him so incredibly sad.

CHAPTER SIX

Nevertheless, Marie and I tried to keep the King happy as much as we could, so the celebrations we planned at Versailles grew larger in scope and more elaborate. But it was one of the birthday parties that we threw for Louis that became one of the most talked about events at court, a festivity that also changed my life forever.

Marie and I spent months planning the perfect fete for our King's 54th birthday. We spared no expense as every florist, musician, singer, dancer and actor in the country that we could find received an invitation to serve as entertainment, with a promised salary that they could not resist. We spent countless hours discussing decor, making sure that even the curtains in the grand ballroom and connected hallways would match the vision of what we had in mind.

We fulfilled our grand plans. Although the King's birthday fell in the wintry month of February, we transformed the Palace into a spring garden, filling it with flowers and plants imported from all over the world. The castle was in full bloom, with grand floral displays set up in well-warmed rooms that made it seem as if the sun had come inside to play with us. There was light everywhere, thanks to the fortune we spent on candles. We set up servants in strategic locations to make sure that if one lit candle burned itself out, another quickly took its place.

Our efforts were not for naught: not only were the guests enamored of our creation, but even Louis remarked about feeling better when he made his way down one of the palace's hallways and into the ballroom. For the first time in months, the King addressed me with a smile and kissed my hand as he might have when he was younger and still had hope within his heart.

Guests from everywhere mingled in the palace's rooms and halls, including old friends and dignitaries from those countries we held alliances with. This included Austria, who sent a cavalcade of nobles to celebrate with us. These men and women entertained us with traditional Bavarian music and even brought some of their chefs along to work in our kitchens to prepare some of their specialties, such as schnitzel, potato dumplings and apple kuchen. They rallied us with stories from their heritage, beautiful fairy tales full of love and romance.

One of those Austrians was a nobleman named Victor Dragomir. I quickly became aware of his existence after his presentation to the King: Victor made himself known to me by catching my eye and winking at me. It was a bold gesture, especially considering my position as King's mistress, but no one in the room seemed to notice this transgression. This seemed a moment that passed only between myself and him.

At first, I was furious at his audacity, but that quickly led to intrigue when I realized something incredibly important about him. I still do not know how I recognized that he was also a vampyr, but it was almost as if the word was written on his high forehead. He was like me, and he was the only other like me that I had ever met.

I was suddenly not alone in my secret, although I often thought that there were others like me out there somewhere, those who possessed the blood disease. But I had grown so accustomed to "normal" life that was only interrupted by my occasional feedings that I often let myself forget what I was.

Victor's appearance at Versailles, though, changed that.

Once I had a spare moment away from chatty nobles and the King, who busied himself discussing politics with the Austrian dignitaries, I sought out the whereabouts of Monsieur Dragomir. Early on, he disappeared from the ballroom, so I began to quietly question the servants about his whereabouts. One of the Austrian staff members told me that he decided to wander into the garden, to enjoy a stroll in the chill winter air.

I quickly sent off one of my servants to fetch a fur shawl for me. When it arrived, I hastily threw it over my shoulders and exited the palace when no one was looking. As my footsteps hurriedly carried me to the garden, fireworks began to go in the dark sky above me. Although several guests stood outside watching the spectacle, most stayed behind the warm windows of the palace, watching them from within.

I ran for the rose garden, fueled by curiosity and instinct. It was almost as if I already knew where I would find this other vampyr, almost as if the creature inside of me knew how to find one of its own.

It was a cold night. A harsh and bitter wind blew against my cheeks, flushing my face and making my lips feel numb. I did not stop, though, at least not until I saw the figure of a man admiring the bare rose bushes. He seemed deep in thought.

I stopped myself just short of where he could see me and stared. He was almost otherworldly, with hair as blonde as mine, his strong cheekbones and jaw lending his face authority. He appeared about my age, but his stature hinted that he was much older than what he physically seemed. The face was young, but the eyes, carefully staring at the bare bushes, spoke of a wisdom far beyond his years.

I had spent years wondering if the myths about vampires being immortal were actually true. I had already noticed that as I grew older, my face did not, even at 40 years of age, that time when women start to fret about wrinkles and dark spots. It seemed that aging slowed down for our kind and that I might live a very long life. But only after I saw Victor musing over the dead garden did I understand that we were immortal. I also suddenly knew that he had knowledge that I needed to possess.

I thought to announce my presence, perhaps with a clearing of my throat, but he seemed to sense me and turned around and spoke first, a smile pressed upon his lips that warmed my cold heart. He bowed deeply, in a manner that was entirely too old-fashioned and said, "Madame."

I was without words, unable to open my mouth to say anything to this man who held the secrets to everything I had ever wanted to know. I felt the ice cage inside of me begin to melt, thanks to the vibrant and alive nature of the man standing before me.

I began to feel things again, and this time, it was more real than anything that I had ever felt before. I thawed in that frozen garden, droplets of water falling from my heart to warm my blood.

Victor stood straight and held out a hand.

Without thinking, I placed my small hand in his larger one.

He turned my hand over and kissed it, although his eyes remained fixed upon my face.

He was presumptous and flirtatious, everything he should not have been to the King's mistress. I did not care.

A cold breeze caressed the back of my neck beneath my fur shawl, causing me to shiver. Tiny flakes of snow began flitting from the sky, landing in my hair, on my dress and at our feet.

"Madame, if I may?" Victor asked, offering me his arm. "I fear we should get you indoors so that you don't catch the cold of your life."

I laughed, because I knew that he was making a joke. As I knew that he was a vampire, he also knew that I was one, too. And our kind never caught a cold, or any other kind of sickness, save for that illness that struck us when we do not feed.

When I laughed, he joined me with a deep chuckle of his own. It felt as we had known each other our entire lives.

Victor walked with me back to the palace, even as the fireworks continued to go off in colorful bangs above our heads, in spite of the snow, in spite of the night. When we reached the palace doors, I waved off the servants waiting for me there, as I continued to cling to Victor's arm. I suddenly felt a desire for nearness to him. My warming heart wanted him more than anything I had ever wanted in my life.

"I will escort Madame de Pompadour inside before the cold claims her," Victor explained to the servants, his French accented with a German accent. This was, again, presumptious of him, and yet, those around us responded to the authority lent in his voice. He was a man used to getting his way, even in a foreign land. It was almost as if he were the ruler of the palace, rather than Louis, thanks to the confident air with which he carried himself. The servants moved out of the way as Victor escorted me back into Versailles, leading me away from the grand ballroom and towards the nearest hallway, a grand long hall filled with art, paintings and sculptures.

We stopped halfway down the hallway. Victor took time to stare at a painting of me, one of the first portraits commissioned by the King after my arrival at the palace. The portrait was lit only by candlelight and showed myself as a young woman, not much different than the woman of 40 years that now stood before it.

Victor stared at the portrait, rubbing his chin. "Madame, I must confess that this portrait does you no favors."

I blinked, not understanding his meaning.

He snickered under his breath before turning his head, his icy blue eyes settling upon my face. "I only meant that it is beautiful, yes, but not as beautiful as the real thing."

Every word that he uttered dripped of charisma. My heart leapt within my chest as I brought one clasped hand to my bosom. I looked down and actually blushed, "Merci, monsieur."

"I still quite like it, though," he remarked as he reached out and touched the painting, his eyes never leaving my face. He took a step closer to me. "It is an elegant reminder of the woman behind the beauty."

I felt his breath tickling my forehead as he stood over me. He smelled of musk and blood, a scent that only another vampire would recognize.

"But now, I feel hungry," he said, licking his lips.

My own hunger and what I was came to life with his words, with that gesture. My attraction to him became something tangible, pressing against me.

"As am I," I replied, daring to move closer to him. "Should I... send for something?"

Victor's lips curled into a smile, a playful and devilish grin that looked at home on his handsome face. "Yes." He placed his hands at my waist and pulled me even closer until I could feel the warmth seeping from his body.

I lifted my hands and laced them around the back of his neck as we kissed. My heart fluttered more than the fireworks that still played their certain kind of music outside.

It was foolish and reckless, my behavior. But I did not care. I allowed the kiss to last for what felt like forever and still tasted him upon my lips long after.

My heart continued to beat in an increasingly faster rhythm as I grew ever bolder. "My room is just above the king's apartments," I whispered, my eyes still half-closed. "Meet me there." Louis was to stay with Marie that night, although I knew that he would probably choose to spend the evening alone, as was becoming his custom.

I finally stepped away from Victor, one hand still placed against his chest.

Victor re-adjusted my fur cape around my shoulders. "Comme tu le souhaitez." As you wish.

As I wished indeed.

As we parted ways, I felt everything inside of me begin to shift. I quickly made my way to my apartments to find my servants as Victor returned to the ballroom to keep up appearances. I felt giddy at our shared secret.

This was a dangerous game I played, and I knew that. Louis was not a jealous man, but still considered me as his property. My young heart desired freedom, though, and I knew that Victor and these new overwhelming feelings would give that to me. Victor was not just my potential soulmate, but could also become my lover, teacher and mentor. These were gifts that even the King of France could not offer me.

My slippered feet carried me away to my rooms as if I walked on air. I quickly gave instructions to my two most trusted servants, those placed in my care by my mother before her passing, who eagerly left in search of two victims, instead of my usual one.

I thought briefly of how disappointed Mother would find my behavior. But I also knew that I was grown now and that it was time to live life a life that was just for me.

My trusted staff, who implicitly understood my needs and quietly took care of them, soon returned with two gifts, a man and woman, presumably a couple, who thought they had won some grand prize to have a special meeting with the Royal Mistress. I instructed them to wait just outside of my apartments, noting that they were both nervous and excited. Meanwhile, the servants spruced up the room as I waited for Victor to join me.

They left food out on a table for me and my guests, although it hardly seemed necessary. Although I, personally, did occasionally indulge in physical food, I did not require it. I did enjoy the taste of certain things, though. Soon, my chamber was full of small platters of produce imported from all over the world, including cranberries, cucumbers and melons. There was also cheese and bread, two things a good French citizen would never live without.

I paced the room as I waited, wondering what was coming over me. I was more anxious than the couple waiting just outside my doors, flitting around the room like a teenager. I thought I had once known love, at least when I was younger, but this was something else, something far more primal. Victor and I were a natural pairing, perhaps even a partnership made of desperation: two vampires who now knew that they were no longer alone in the world.

But if Victor existed, wouldn't that mean there were also others like us? I had so many questions, but my thoughts continued to return to the feel of Victor's kiss upon my lips. Just the thought of it made me short of breath, barely able to breathe, remembering what it felt like when I put my arms around him.

A knock on the door signaled his arrival. I quickly instructed the servants to allow him, and our intended victims, entrance into the room. As I waited for them to enter, I cut myself a slice of Camembert and pinched off a small piece of bread, eating it, but not tasting it.

My body was on pins and needles, every nerve alert in my body. I tingled with anticipation.

I heard the outer apartment doors open and then close. I hurriedly chewed my food and sat down on the edge of my bed, facing the door, my hands delicately placed in my lap. I seemed poised and far more patient than I felt. I listened to the sounds of footsteps crossing through the rooms towards where I waited.

Victor, followed by the couple, stepped into the room. I stood up and nodded to him, gesturing for the couple to join us. Victor returned the nod, a soft smile placed on his lips. We needed no words.

In that moment, I saw Victor for the man I thought he was. I was regal, yes, but he was something even more: noble, yes, but also a little renegade. And that excited me as much as the beautiful shock of white blonde hair that lay above his handsome brow.

If the intended victims felt that something was afoot, they did not show it. Instead, they waited patiently for introductions. But there were none. The man, who stood at Victor's side, did not even see when Victor lunged at him with abandon. The woman with did not even have time to react as I threw myself upon her. As I reached into my bosom and pulled out my little knife, the last reminder of my mother, I saw Victor pull a ceremonial dagger from a scabbard tied around his waist. We sliced across our victims' necks in synchronicity and began to drink.

Our mouths found instant purchase upon those arteries, blood gushing into our mouths, warm, hot and coppery, down our throats.

My belly warmed as I drank, my eyes never leaving Victor's. We shuffled our feet until we stood close to each other, drinking our fill, our gazes locked in a heated exchange. Blood slipped from my mouth and splashed across my dress and on to the floor. Blood dripped from Victor's lips and down his chin.

We stood side by side, drinking, indulging in something far more intimate than foreplay.

Victor dropped the man's body to the floor and licked his crimson lips.

I did the same and groaned deeply, my body full of lust.

We embraced, our mouths hungrily finding each other. I tasted blood on his lips. He tasted blood on mine. We kissed, our tongues lashing at each other as if in battle, desperate and needy. I prayed that he would never release me.

With one hand, Victor grabbed my dress at the top of the bodice and ripped it, its seams falling apart under his strong grip. His hands deftly untied the corset strings underneath, freeing my torso from confinement. One warm hand reached up to touch my cold breast, a thumb carefully teasing and caressing the nipple.

I fell into his arms, almost as if in a swoon, with one hand reaching up, clinging to his shirt. This was not Romeo and Juliet, at all, but Antony and Cleopatra. This was a mature lust and it felt so good.

Victor made quick work of undressing me, while also slipping out of his own articles of clothing. We stood naked above a pile of clothes, two vampires who just happened to meet on that particular night.

His hands quietly guided me to the bed. As he pressed me down against the duvet, he began leaving trails of kisses across my porcelain body. I grabbed at him, feeling my own strength build, flipping us over so that I straddled him. I brought him inside of me and we moved to a rhythm that was all our own, two immortal creatures in perfect harmony. Our love-making was both gentle and violent at the same time.

When we were spent, we lay relaxed, spread out across many bulky pillows, the bedclothes wrinkled beneath us, my long blond hair undone and spread across his chest. Victor held me with one arm, his hand gently caressing my shoulder.

I was no stranger to sex, but this went beyond that. This was a connection made with my own kind, something I could never experience with a mere human.

We lay like that for some time before either of us spoke a word. I felt something continue to shift inside of me. Change was on the horizon.

Hours passed as the candles that lit the room extinguished, leaving only moonlight streaming through the bedroom's window. Victor finally broke the silence. "Tomorrow, I will hire an artist to paint you," he whispered as he kissed the top of my forehead. "That is my wish."

"Yes," I replied, wanting to do whatever it took to please him. This frightened me, once I realized that. No man ever had such power over me, at least emotionally, not since Philippe. But this man was different. *I* was different, forever changed having met one of my own.

"Are you happy here?" Victor asked, changing the subject as his fingertips played with tendrils of my hair.

I stopped myself from saying that I was. Because that was a lie. I no longer had to please Mother. I no longer had to please fate. So I answered honestly, "No." Uttering the word made me realize its truth. This was never the life I wanted, but the life that my Mother wanted for me. And for so long, I believed that she knew best. But that was then: now I knew I was not alone with this blood disease, with this human evolution that made me a vampire.

But there was also more. In my newly awakened emotional state, I said something I never thought I would say to another man. "Take me with you?" I whispered, almost afraid as if he might hear me. "Take me to Austria." After I muttered the words, though, I realized their truth. Versailles no longer felt like home.

Victor laughed, but there was something strange in his tone, something I would remember later. "What about the King?" he asked.

I slowly shook my head. "I am nearly 40. Louis grows tired of me." Although the truth was that Louis grew tired with the world. "I grow tired of him. And I do not age, and soon, others will notice that. I think, perhaps, my time at court has come to an end."

"You cannot just pick up and leave," Victor stated, as he lifted his hand in front of his face to regard it in the moonlight. "The King wouldn't allow it. I know this, because if I were him, I would never let you leave my presence."

I blushed, wishing more than ever that this night would never end.

"But I can help you... escape, if that is truly what you wish," he continued as he pulled himself up on one elbow to regard me. He touched my breast, which responded to his fingertips. I felt that familiar thrill rush through me as his other hand brushed through my hair, slightly tugging on it. Goosebumps crossed my flesh as my heart began beating fast again.

There were no thought processes needed in my answer. This was something I always knew must happen eventually. I could not stay at Versailles forever. There were already rumors about how my beauty never faded, although the years passed on. At the age of 40, I still resembled a girl of 19. I could not let them know me for what I was because they would not understand it. And people feared and hated what they did not understand. If I could bow out now, at the height of my career as a mistress, then my good name, and my mother's legacy - something I still somewhat cared about - would live on.

"It is what I wish," I responded.

"Then we will make certain arrangements," he replied as he pulled his body on top of mine. "And you will come with me, Madame." His hand traced the length of my breastbone and wandered further down, finding that place between my legs.

I responded immediately, my back arching, the taste of blood still remembered upon my lips.

Our lovemaking was quieter and slower this second time, and remained so throughout the night. Sensations like I had never known rolled over my body again and again. And this could really go on forever. I was immortal. Victor was immortal. Time was now a friend, something I would always have on my side.

Outside, snow drifted lazily past the window panes. Winter was here, but my life was a never-ending summer. Madame de Pompadour would live on and she would become something more.

Just before sleep overtook me, my thoughts drifted to a future that suddenly became more clear. The world was mine! And instead of wasting it away at Versailles, I could leave this place and go out into that world and do something with this extraordinary life I was born into. I would see the rise and fall of empires and be witness to what others would only read about in books.

Goodnight, sweet Victor, I thought to myself, as my eyes closed and I drifted off to sleep.

CHAPTER SEVEN

My time with Louis diminished more in the following weeks, even after the wonderful birthday party we threw in his honor. His depression hung like a pall over the palace, a gray cloud that affected everyone who resided within. The King seemed to have no hope left for France and no hope left for himself. There were rumors that he succumbed to madness, stories about how he preferred the company of his pet squirrel over people, that he spent many hours talking to the animal as it were counsel. I found that I no longer wanted to spend time in his presence, especially now that I had a new happiness settling within my heart.

I coped by spending more time with Victor. At court, the two of us only seemed as friends, two people who seemed to share an affiliation for the same books, the same art and the same music. At night, though, under the cover of darkness, we were lovers, entangled in each others' limbs. I found such joy in his body and his ways.

Victor was also something else: he was my second chance at love. Although I had long ago put aside the incident with Philippe, I did find a new understanding of what that word "love," "amour" actually meant. The love I had for Philippe was that of a child, the kind of love that doesn't even begin to understand matters of the heart and head. My feelings for Victor were something more, the stuff not of poems, but of great epic tales of lovers who find each other after so many years.

As the days passed, I began to grow more weary of Versailles. The thought of leaving pressed upon me. I was no longer of use to the King, and I desired to crawl out from under the weight of Louis and his oppressive melancholy. I longed to find a new freedom outside of anything I had ever known before.

Victor and I began to plan my exit from court. The only way I could legitimately leave the palace was by a decree from the King or by death. But Louis would not entertain talk of my leaving: he still insisted that I remain close, which I did, because I was still no more than something he owned, another toy he had grown tired of, but could not bear to part with.

So my escape could only come with my death. This was the only way I could ever leave Versailles. But I was immortal, and would probably not die, at least not of natural causes and not anytime soon.

As a vampire, it is true that death is always around the corner, and Victor was the first to inform me that our kind could truly die, but never of old age. It was possible to kill us, although that was also difficult because our bodies proved stronger than those of mortals.

It was my love for theatre and my penchant for acting that finally offered me a way out. I must pretend to grow ill and die. I would not really pass on, but I could arrange to have myself declared dead. And after a long feigned illness, no one would question it.

Such a scheme would never work in the modern age, but at the time, it was the perfect plan.

Victor and I began to take steps to put my plan into place. To make myself seem ill, I stopped feeding, one of the most difficult things I ever had to do in my life. I took no blood for several months and after doing so, I actually did become sick. It was much like the illness that held me in its thrall in my childhood before I learned what I was. I became weak and barely responsive, but in my few lucid moments, I reminded myself that this was for a purpose, a means to an end to secure my freedom, although I craved blood with every part of my being.

I spent my days bedridden, staring at the same light blue wallpaper every day, its golden fleur de lys pattern taunting me and swirling before my clouded eyes. I held firm, though, in maintaining my fast as I huddled under many fur blankets, trembling from a cold that no one else felt, in spite of the constant fire in my fireplace.

During this time, I saw Louis more than I had in the past few years. He grew concerned about my condition and sent for doctors, but although they were learned men of science, they never uncovered the true cause of my illness. But they were all certain of one thing: I was dying.

Louis sent for priests to pray over me, but little did they know that my "death" was inevitable. Not because that is the nature of death, but because I had planned it that way.

Victor told me that he once saw the King weep over me during one of his visits. I am not sure if Victor said this in being kind or if Louis really did mourn for the decline of my health. I felt a small pang of guilt in my deceit, but common sense told me that this was my only path in moving on. This would assure that, I am immortal, would never get faced with questions about why my beauty never faded and why I never aged. I had to preserve my reputation, but I also had to leave Versailles as I was now and never look back.

As the "illness" took me, I became too weak to even carry out the rest of the plan. I depended on Victor to make all the proper arrangements, trusting him fully to see to the details that were necessary after my "demise." He helped me set aside bank accounts filled with assets that would always assure my wealth. He worked out plans with the King for my funeral and burial, with the demand that my body be laid to rest in Paris.

He also sat beside me every day for hours, reading to me and holding my hand, still gazing at me as if my beauty weren't tainted by my lack of feeding. I was still pretty, of course, but my cheeks became sallow and sunken in, my flaxen hair lost its luster, my eyes grew cloudy, lines grew around the edges of my mouth, I was also too thin and my usual guarded smile became a grimace because of the pain that constantly wracked me. Every bone and muscle in my body craved blood and I often thought that, at times, death really would come soon to claim me.

A great fever came over me and brought about crazy dreams, which often featured appearances by my dead mother.

Perhaps it was because I realized that I was leaving her behind in wanting to leave Versailles: in those dreams she always stared at me with disappointment. When I reached out to her in these hallucinations for one last mother and daughter embrace, she would disappear. I often woke up weeping, although my body barely had the energy to produce tears.

I hated myself like this, but again, I was determined to redraw my fate.

I slept a lot during that time and many of those days became a blur. There were servants interrupting my sleep by shoving spoonfuls of broth into my mouth and doctors attaching leeches to my body. But everything was like a drug-induced haze, and I began to confuse reality and dreams. I recall that Marie visited me occasionally, usually having tea served in my room, but I was too weak to lift a cup to my lips or enjoy her visits.

As a woman who prided herself on strength, I felt some shame. I, the great Madame de Pompadour, was now reduced to this shell of a thing.

During my sickness, though, I learned something important about the French court: My sorry state turned me into a pigeon surrounded by cats. Some of my strongest opponents often visited me, often with fake nice words, even as they quietly prayed for my death. I felt their presence, as well as their hatred, when they turned up, but I would never allow it to affect me, not even in my weakened state. Because I seemed incapable of thought, they would often admit their hatred to me aloud, knowing that I was in no condition to do anything about it. I usually feigned sleep, but my mind remained active and I quietly noted all their names.

I was not one to act on revenge, but knowing one's enemies, even in death, seemed important. And sometimes, I managed to come out of my stupor just long enough to have Victor write down the names of those who wronged me. Victor would then, in turn, offer those names to the King.

Madame de Pompadour was dying, but she was not gone yet.

After months of my illness, it was time for me to die, or at least appear dead. Before, though, there was one last visit from

Louis. I managed to utter a few words about my final wishes.

Louis patted my hand as I made him promise to see to my burial in Paris, as I made him promise that there would be no big event heralding my passing. "Mon cheri, you are going nowhere," he told me. "I will not allow it." His deep eyes, though, dotted with unwept tears said their silent goodbye. That was the last I saw of the King.

The next day, Victor had a doctor declare me dead. It was a simple process: I merely held my breath while the physician checked to see if I still breathed. Then, several servants dressed me in one of my finest dresses, a gown of lavender silk and lace, and placed my body into an elaborate golden coffin, a parting gift from the King. Per my requests, there was no huge ceremony. Servants loaded the heavy coffin into a beautiful carriage bound for Paris. From my place of rest, I heard the first rumbles of thunder as Louis' voice whispered, "La marquise n'aura pas de beau temps pour son voyage."

Large drops pounded against the carriage as it began its journey down the King's road away from Versailles and my old life. About halfway along the route to Paris, the carriage stopped before an obstacle, another carriage blocking the road. After my driver left my vehicle to investigate, Victor emerged from behind the second carriage and attacked him, slitting his throat. Then Victor broke into my wooden coffin and threw the body at me. The scent of fresh blood brought life back to my dying limbs, giving me just enough strength to lift my weak body up and cover the man's open wound with my mouth. As I drank, my breathing evened and my cheeks plumped out, the wrinkles around my eyes disappeared and my body returned to a healthy state.

We placed the carriage driver's body in my cheap wooden coffin and resealed it. One of Victor's servants would continue driving that carriage to Paris and deliver the coffin to the Couvent des Capucines, my chosen burial place.

To this day, that man remains buried deep beneath Paris in my stead.

Victor gave me a change of clothes and helped me into a second carriage. After stepping inside, I noticed a painting leaning against one of the walls of the coach. I recognized it immediately: it was the portrait from Versailles, the one Victor remarked upon shortly after our first meeting. I believed it a reminder: Victor had stolen the heart of the King's mistress, along with her portrait.

We desperately made love within the confines of the vehicle as his driver whisked us out of France. In my illness, I had missed the feel of Victor's body against mine and the way our skin glimmered in the moonlight. I craved his touch, which was both delicate and violent. My new life began anew, there in Victor's arms.

As we crossed the border out of France and into Germany, I stared out of the carriage window, noting the snow-capped mountains of Bavaria. The countryside was quiet, hushed, and the air was clean and crisp. As dawn awoke the world, I saw a large flock of black birds flying noiselessly above us.

Those birds represented my freedom, I believed. Victor had given me a gift that not even my mother could provide: a life of my own.

Such was my life and my death. My journey continued.

CHAPTER EIGHT

A s we traveled, we took refuge in small inns for sleeping. News of my death seemed to reach across Europe, and I was careful to hide my face behind a veil whenever we were in public. My fame surprised me, although more often than not, many uttered "good riddance" under their breath when mention of me came up in conversation.

The people who greeted our arrival in Austria were simple, dirty, uneducated and superstitious. Every man, woman and child wore a cross around their neck, often with a small bulb of garlic. They often randomly made the sign of the evil eye. It was such a change from the elite educated society that I was so used to that I began to miss the cultured part of the world that was once my home. Versailles had never seemed so far away.

But although I felt far away from home, I remained committed to my decision to leave my beloved France. I was also curious about the rest of the world, especially now that I would get to see it. I was a free woman in a time when most women never were. Through my slight sadness, I felt liberated.

There was also the hope that I would someday return to France. My leaving was temporary, something to give time a chance to erase at least part of the country's memories of me.

Our carriage rolled through small Austrian villages dotted with its superstitious people before arriving at Bran Castle, one of many properties owned by Victor. I already understood that Victor was a man of means, but the chateau still impressed me when I first saw it in the distance. The castle was in the middle of the Alps, where it sat high on top of one of the snow-capped mountains, towering above many of the range's highest peaks.

It reminded me of some of the castles of the Loire Valley, but was even more magnificent, a beautiful thing made of stone with many turrets and towers.

The carriage pulled us along a narrow pathway that wound around a steep mountain range, a feat that left our horses tired and out of breath. Once we got closer, I found myself in awe of my new home. As the carriage stopped in front of the castle's main gates, I took a moment to prepare myself for the new life that would begin the moment I stepped outside.

The carriage door opened and I took the driver's hand, carefully arranging my skirts as I exited the vehicle. I looked up, but saw nothing but gray towers looming over me, the sky blocked out by the castle's exterior. I barely noticed when Victor took my hand and led me up a short flight of steps and into the building itself.

The interior was just as impressive. Old tapestries hung on the walls telling of battles lost and won. A smell of must mixed with flowers lingered in the air. A bevy of servants attended to large hearths, a group of locals not like the ones we previously encountered. These people did not possess crosses or garlic. They did not make the sign of the evil eye when Victor and I drew close. These were Victor's loyal servants, probably aware of what he was, probably members a family that had served Victor over lifetimes.

This was my new home. These were my people. I began to imagine living hundreds of years in that castle having all my needs taken care of, while Victor taught me everything I needed to know about being a *vampyr*.

As we entered the castle's main grand hall, servants lined up on two sides to meet us and bowed with reverence. One of the younger servants, a girl of around 16 years, approached me with a bouquet of white roses. I took the bouquet and thanked her before she scurried off to join the others.

I marveled as Victor walked me up a large circular staircase to what would become my bedroom. Although darkness began to fall outside, the castle was well-lit with burning candles flaring from every wall sconce and within every candlestick. Their flickering fire gave the evening a magical feel, as if this were surreal, as if I were experiencing this outside of my body. It was all so new and exciting that when we reached my room, my breath caught in my throat.

The room itself was exquisite. It was more extravagant and larger than my apartments at Versailles. A mahogany rug sat atop a burnished wood floor. Above that, a delicately carved wooden four-poster bed enticed me to lay upon it and fall asleep. A beautiful gold brocade fabric made up the bedclothes and canopy. The scent of lavender filled the room. My porcelain collection, shipped from Versailles, was in a large display cabinet, with other pieces strewn about the room as decor. It was perfect, a testament that Victor had spared no thought or cost into making me feel welcome here.

After allowing me time to gain my bearings, Victor finally spoke, giving me my first instructions, "You will not harm the servants. Take and feed upon as many of the villagers as you like, but I have promised the servants safety from our kind."

This seemed perfectly reasonable, so I nodded, intent on keeping to the agreement. *"D'accord, mon cherie,"* I answered.

Victor smiled and bowed and made his exit, leaving me alone to collect my thoughts.

As I sat down on the bed, feeling weary from the long journey, servants rushed to my aid to assist me in taking off my shoes. They washed my feet, their eyes never gazing up at my face. They were dutiful to their master, and now to me, as I was now, also under his charge and their care. They helped me out of my wrinkled traveling clothes and chose a beautiful gown of the richest scarlet velvet to dress me in for dinner.

It might surprise some that vampires do enjoy things as human as dinner, and perhaps it is even more surprising that we do enjoy food, even if it does not provide us the nutrition that we require. But we still find delight in the taste of a well-served meal, as well as the robust flavor of a good wine.

After dressing me, the servants led me back down the long circular staircase and through the grand foyer to a massive dining room. A long table sat in the center of the room, surrounded by matching chairs. There were portraits on the walls of men in uniform: upon closer inspection, I realized that one of those men was Victor. I was about to remark upon it before a servant interrupted my thoughts and directed me to my seat, which sat to the left of Victor's, at the head of the table.

Then, servants brought out a feast, beginning with a stew of lamb, potatoes and carrots. I ate a full serving, but I remained hungry. The journey was a long one and I was still undernourished from my long illness at Versailles.

"One moment," Victor said as he held up a slender index finger.

A servant came to attention behind him.

"Madame de Pompadour..." Victor began.

I interrupted him. "I am no longer Madame of anything. I am merely Reinette." I found pride in my newfound freedom.

Victor smiled, the thin line of his lips curling up in wry pleasure. He addressed the servant. "Reinette would like dessert now," he told the man, snapping his fingers.

The servant disappeared.

I waited patiently as I wondered what Victor was up to.

Several minutes passed in quiet, but the servant eventually reappeared holding a covered silver tray between his hands. From beneath the tray's cover, I heard the distinctive sound of a baby cooing.

I blinked, shocked, even as an excitement tickled me from deep within, something similar to what I felt when I tasted blood for the first time.

The servant placed the tray on the table in front of me and stood behind my chair, awaiting further instructions.

Victor stood and motioned for the servant to take his leave.

The servant obliged. There was no expression on the man's face: he was blank, as if this were all standard procedure.

Victor gestured to the tray, as if to hurry me into unveiling my surprise.

I placed my napkin down into my lap. I bit my lip hard, drawing blood. I was a little nervous and frightened, but also boiling over with anticipation. I grabbed the cover of the tray and lifted it up. Upon it lay a chubby baby. Its eyes were half-closed and it made a quiet little chirping noise.

My stomach leapt into my throat as I placed the cover on the table beside the tray.

"Drugged," Victor explained.

I knew what he expected of me. I procured my small knife from my bosom and held it tightly in my hand just above where the baby lay on the tray.

"Bon appetit," Victor stated, his smile growing into a grin that nearly took over his entire face.

In that moment, I briefly entertained the notion that he was insane. But I did not care. Love... or lust... or infatuation... never sees such things.

I licked my lips as I carefully picked the child up, cradling it in the crook of one elbow. With my free hand, which held the knife, I made a small slice against the child's throat. My arms trembled as I brought the infant's neck to my lips. *I should not do this*, I told myself, but something more primal drowned that voice out.

The baby's blood tasted like the sweetest nectar, unlike anything I had tasted before. It was the pure essence of life, full of promise, joy and potential. I drank and drank until I felt its tiny, yet strong, heart finally give.

Once sated, I carefully lay the baby back down on the tray. I swooned, its blood leaving me feeling drunk and light-headed.

Victor's voice came from somewhere on my right, barely cutting through the ecstasy I floated in. "Are you pleased, my lady?" he asked.

I nodded, unable to answer.

Victor excused himself from dinner before me, stating that he had matters to attend to and that he would join me later.

When I retired to my bedroom that evening, servants undressed me and helped me get into bedclothes. I dismissed them quickly and lay on the bed, staring at the canopy above me. I felt more sated and alive than ever. That a small thing could bring me such joy and such sustenance should have caused me a greater measure of guilt than I experienced, but it did not. Others might judge the act with pure disgust, calling me a criminal, or even referring to me as a monster. But I was beginning to understand that I was not any of these things. I merely was.

Victor arrived a few hours later, pleased and still smiling, as if ready to devour me in a single bite. As he threw himself on top of me and ripped away my gown, I opened myself up to him and let myself go, screaming his name over and over in exultation, uncaring who heard. This, too, was a new level of freedom.

I had lived and I had died. And now, I lived again. Exhaustion led me to fall asleep quickly, dreamless and still.

No longer trapped by fears and inhibitions, of locked up emotions, I felt free. I no longer worried about religion or society or what was nice, good or even safe. I was free from morality, free from judgment, free to find myself, free to become the thing I was born to be. I finally became that evolved being my mother always saw in me, a creature that depended on the cycle of life as surely as a lioness hunts and eats a gazelle. But I was the lion, and humans were my prey. It was natural. It was me.

My very thought processes began to change. I was no longer human, although I physically possessed many human qualities. I let that little part of my humanity that remained slip away as I became something more, something better.

Mother would have been so proud.

Although Victor did not present me with another infant after that first night, he still brought me a delectable treat each week. Once, it was a feisty local boy, who cursed at me in Romanian as I drank. Several times, I would get orphans that Victor found roaming the countryside. Sometimes, it was a woman. Sometimes, it was a man. I did not go hungry at Bran Castle. And I did not care who I drank from, only that I drank. I also did not drink because I needed it, but because I enjoyed it. I enjoyed that intimate taking of life. It gave me a sense of power and soon became my drug, my addiction.

The world was now open to me in an entirely different way.

CHAPTER NINE

It only took several months of joy, though, before my time in the castle became routine. While at Versailles, I was always busy, either philosophizing with some of the greatest minds in the world or planning grand fetes with Marie at my side. Now, I had none of that, nor any duties to anyone other than myself. There was no King to please or artists to visit with or scholars to debate the state of France with.

Although once obsessed with fashion, I found the dressmakers of Austria relatively uninspired. I began to shun my gowns, save for dinner, for men's clothes. I often wore breeches, shirts and vests. I found this apparel far less restrictive than my grand gowns and corsets and discovered some liberation in being able to wear such things without anyone judging me for it. Victor only complimented me and told me I was even more beautiful dressed as a man and he took as much pleasure in undressing me when I was in pants than when I wore skirts. The servants would never dare to criticize and the people in the village simply did not care as they kept their distance.

This newfound freedom, though, also meant that I had no sense of purpose. I spent some days wandering around the village, but the locals often hissed and cursed at me under their breath, making the sign of the evil eye any time I stepped into a shop to admire a hat or piece of fabric or trim. I was a foreigner in a strange land.

At times, my freedom seemed almost as much of a cage as being the King's mistress.

Victor also spent less time with me. Instead, he returned to his "studies." Although he never spoke of them, I only understood that he indulged himself in some sort of intellectual laboratory work in the large network of tunnels and rooms underneath the castle that made up its basement. But this work began to consume him most days and late into the evenings.

By my fourth month at Bran Castle, the honeymoon was over.

I begged Victor to show me his work, this thing that he was so passionate about. I wanted to become a part of it, as well as give myself something to do, something that might give my life meaning. But he stayed secretive and would never offer up many details, although he did eventually admit to me that he was studying us, vampires. He wanted to learn about the scientific secret held in our special blood. He wanted to discover what anomaly created us and why it made us different. He wanted to know why we existed.

To me, this sounded like an honorable pursuit, and when he often chose that over me, I supported him. What more could I do?

Curiosity, though, is a strange little bird that whispers in your ear little secrets that make you crave more, so much that you feel you might die without knowledge of everything. That curiosity is like a train that, once it has left the station, speeds up and only slows down and stops once it reaches its destination, that place where you want to go. I knew where I wanted to go. I wanted to know more.

As a diplomat for his country, Victor occasionally left Austria to visit with other dignitaries. And it was upon such an occasion that I set a plan in place to begin gathering more knowledge about his research.

With Victor gone, the basement of the quiet and lonely castle became unguarded. Victor trusted me, though, so perhaps I felt some small ounce of guilt at my planned betrayal, at something that made me feel as if I were abandoning his trust. But wasn't he the one keeping secrets from me? Had I not shared all with him, my body and soul, and should I not know everything about him in return?

Victor kept the basement laboratory locked, and he usually wore the key around his neck. Before he left, though, I watched him hand the key off to a servant, a man by the name of Klaus. When I requested it, though, Klaus did not want to give up the key so easily. The only way I could claim it was to break the first rule that Victor ever gave me: I killed the man and took the key for myself. After, I buried the body, leaving no trace, and when other servants asked for Klaus' whereabouts, I feigned ignorance. And I would do the same when Victor returned.

Was it foolish? Perhaps. Was it dangerous? Absolutely. But I needed to know about the work that often kept my lover from me.

I did not make my move until several days after Klaus' disappearance. I waited until the servants would not suspect me of foul play, biding my time impatiently. Once I ascertained that they would not watch me, I quickly grabbed a lantern and hurried down the steep set of stairs that led to the basement door. I quietly placed the key in the lock and turned it, hearing that "click" sound signaling that the lock had disengaged. I pushed against the heavy door and stepped inside.

Darkness greeted me, but I found my way to a candelabra and used the lantern to light the candles that it held. It barely made a difference in the cavern-like room that was so damp that droplets of moisture clung to its stone walls. Inside the room, there were a series of tables with glass vials, filled with substances of various colors. There was a large fireplace in the room, filled with burnt logs and ashes that smelled like chemicals and refuse.

I approached a desk that sat in the corner of the room. Littered upon its surface were a series of hand-written pages. I sat in the leather chair behind the desk and picked up the top sheet, lifting the lantern up so that I could read it.

The sheet contained equations, numbers and symbols that I did not understand. I placed it down and shuffled through more pages full of similar writings before noticing a leather-bound book beneath the pile. I picked the book up and opened it to its first page. The handwriting was unmistakable, it was written in German, in Victor's own hand.

"Day One: I am marking my words here in this journal to track progress on the experiments I've begun on the vampire. I have drawn

samples of blood from myself and a human subject and compared them, both heating the samples up and cooling them down. Although there is no difference, the human blood became dry and dark after six hours. However, the vampire blood remained fresh. Perhaps this begins to explain the vampire's immortality."

I turned several pages and kept reading:

"Day 45: The vampire blood remains fresh and seems unaffected by variables added to it. It does not evaporate when heated up, but remains at the same temperature. It does not freeze, but remains liquid, suggesting why heat and cold barely affect vampire kind. But why? What makes this blood so special? Where did this mutation come from?"

I flipped through more pages and continued to read:

"Day 60: I have begun studying the vampire corpse, with a comparison to the human corpse. Upon examination, I discovered remarkable differences between the two bodies' digestive tracts. The human digestive tract leads directly to the stomach, but the vampire's leads to the arteries and then into the heart. This offers an explanation of the vampire lust for blood."

"Day 120: Breakthrough! When human blood comes into contact with vampire blood, the vampire blood consumes the human blood and replaces it with more of itself."

But there was more:

"Day 125: I have attempted to duplicate the experiment with a live human subject. I injected vampire blood into subject A's bloodstream and waited for a response. Unfortunately, the human subject did not survive. It seems that converting a human into a vampire with a vampire's blood is merely a myth."

I turned the pages over, faster and faster, wanting to read more, needing to read more. It suddenly became clear what Victor hoped to accomplish: he wanted to create more of our kind. But that did not make sense because as I understood it, we were born as vampires, weren't we?

"Day 142: I have learned of a vampire at French court. I have seen her portraits. She is very beautiful. Perhaps she will help me follow through with my experiments when the time is right."

These words chilled me, but my hands could not stop turning pages in the journal and my eyes could not stop reading. *"Day 160: Reinette is as lovely as her photos, perhaps more. She is also the perfect candidate for continuing my work. But I fear that I have grown too intimate with her, and now we share an unmistakable bond. Is it because of what we both are? Is it because I am lonely? Is it because I understand what's at stake with my work? What if I am wrong? Will I blame her for my failed science? It is unthinkable, and yet, I cannot bear to live a life without her. My experiment is now a personal one, but it is far too late to change the way I feel. She is a King's mistress, but I, a mere immortal, want to steal her away. So I must have her. She is the day in my world of night."*

The room spun around me I read faster and faster, taking in all the little secrets and lies that led me to where I now stood. And although the words I read gave me pause, they also showed something else, Victor's love for me was powerful: this thought kept me grounded. How could I direct anger at him?

However, I was still a part of his work, in spite of my ignorance of it. Needing to know more, I read on.

"Day 199: Reinette has joined me at the castle, to my delight. Her presence here brings sunlight to this dark and dank place. But I still do not think she is ready to learn of my ideas. I have told her nothing, and the guilt of my dishonesty gnaws at my gut. But there is something else, too, something she has not yet realized. My experiment inadvertently began again, and this time, it seems a success. Reinette is not aware of it yet, but in my attempt to create another vampire, I now believe I have done so. Reinette is with child. I have succeeded where I previously failed."

I stopped reading, looking up to stare at the dark ceiling, the shadows of light and dark playing with each other against its hard surface. The ground beneath me shifted and the room tilted as a wave of dizziness threatened to overcome me. I closed my eyes and focused on my breathing, forcing myself to try and deny what I had just read. I placed a hand on my stomach and rubbed it. I had reason to believe that I was infertile because I was a vampire.

This journal was all lies, or even worse, the musings of a mad man. Vampires could not have babies. I did not even have a monthly cycle. The idea that I carried a child was preposterous.

But the little bird inside my head insisted otherwise. That little bird knew things that I refused to acknowledge myself. When one rules out the impossible, the improbable happens. And although it was very improbable, I knew that I was pregnant with Victor's child.

I do not know how long I sat at Victor's desk staring blankly up at the dark ceiling as I imagined this tiny thing that had begun to grow inside of me. Perhaps I sat there for minutes. Perhaps I sat there for hours. The flickering of the forgotten lamp remained steady, but I was mentally far away from that room.

Eventually, though, a commotion began to occur somewhere above me. I heard Victor calling my name, which forced me back into the moment and into action. I quickly rearranged everything on the desk to leave it as I found it and grabbed the lamp. I ran out of the basement, stopping just long enough to make sure the door locked behind me. My feet swiftly took me back up into the castle proper as I ran to my room. I shoved the laboratory key, still clung tightly in my hand, under my mattress, with thoughts to place it somewhere less conspicuous later.

Victor dashed into the room minutes later and grabbed me before I had a chance to sit down.

He knows, I thought. *He knows that I betrayed his trust.*

"I came as soon as I heard," he said.

This confused me, but I assumed that a servant saw me enter the basement and had alerted him. Perhaps they even saw me read the journal. His attitude, though, was not that of blame, but of concern.

My hand instinctively went to my belly again, imagining the life just underneath the skin and muscle there. I shook my head, my long unbound curls flowing over my shoulders.

"You don't know, do you?" he asked as he pressed his hands against my shoulder and guided me towards the bed. He gently pushed me down so that I would sit. "I was certain someone would inform you." He carefully took my hand and patted it. "I'm sorry, Reinette. The King of France, King Louis, is dead."

One might think his words would affect me differently, but it seems that they only touched something inside of me that was barely there. Did I grieve for the King, the man who was once my lover?

The answer was no. That life, that Reinette, was gone.

I responded by nodding. The only emotion I felt was not for that, but for the written words held in the journal downstairs. I placed one hand over Victor's hand. There was something more important than the King's death. There was this. And there was us.

"And I am with child," I announced.

CHAPTER TEN

Over the months, my belly grew with the child Victor and I created together. I soon learned that a vampire pregnancy was similar to a mortal one, except that there was even more pain, more morning sickness and more swollen feet and ankles.

The phrase "eating for two" took on an entirely new meaning. Before the pregnancy, I only fed a few times a month, but once the child inside me began to grow, I began craving blood more often, nearly every week. Victor did his best to keep me in victims, although we had to move our search beyond the village to prevent the townspeople from growing too suspicious. Many died at my hand for the sake of my baby in those incredibly long months.

Although blood sated myself and my unborn child, I began to have an aversion to its smell and its taste. This made feeding more difficult and it would often take great effort not to vomit up blood after I ingested it. Morning sickness was more of an all-day affair as nausea, dizziness and queasiness claimed me.

As my belly swelled, so did the hell of my pregnancy. The months passed slowly, while I rolled around on my bedsheets in agony, praying for birth to arrive soon. When my water broke in a bloody mess and the first pangs of labor hit me, I found relief, knowing that my ordeal would soon end.

Victor called for a midwife from the village, an older woman with a variety of crosses hanging around her neck. I screamed at her to leave the room. This I would do myself.

She fled the room as soon as my inhuman screaming began. The excruciating pain of birth was a welcome one, though. I pushed through it, as the baby worked its way through my body and into the world. Its screams joined mine as it took air into its lungs for the first time.

Victor cut the umbilical cord himself, knotting it. I watched curiously as he bathed the bloody infant in a basin. When he handed it back to me, I realized that it was a girl, an ugly little thing with a screwed up face and wrinkly form. But it was also mine, delivered from my womb, and because of this, a great love swelled within my bosom as I observed it laying in my arms. But the baby kicked and screamed with more energy than such a small thing should possess, and I realized that it needed to feed.

As a vampire, my breasts were dry, but I knew that it was not milk that the baby hungered for. Therein, lay a dilemma. Victor, though, sprung into action and grabbed the midwife before a carriage could return her to the village. He brought her up to the room with a story that the baby needed medical attention. She crossed herself when she saw the baby, its hungry eyes already focused upon its prize. As the terrified woman turned to leave, Victor caught her by the wrist and made quick work of slicing her arm open with a fingernail, dragging her to where the baby and I lay upon the bed. The old woman's eyes grew wide as I pressed the infant's mouth against her wound.

As Victor held the woman steady, the baby began suckling the blood, its tiny hands clinging to the woman's wrist as a human baby reaches for its mother's breast. The child drank for minutes while the woman sobbed. Soon sated, the infant fell asleep in my arms.

I grabbed the woman and pulled her bleeding wrist to my mouth, draining her. I tossed her to the floor after she died, enjoying a near drug-like stupor, heady from both the blood and the birth.

As Victor dragged the body away, I deducted that his previous theories were right: we could create more vampires, easily, through the very natural process of procreation and childbirth.

Victor, the proud father, re-entered the room and took our daughter in his arms, doting over her. "She needs a name," he insisted as we took turns holding her and cooing at the child under our breaths.

"It must be a good one," I replied.

"Esperanza," Victor said as he stood up and bounced up and down with the baby snuggled over his shoulder, comforting her. I rolled the idea of that name over in my head and it felt right. "Esperanza Antoinette Poisson," I answered, realizing that I wanted the child to have my name, and not his. Perhaps I was already claiming her as my own, as something that belonged more to me than to him.

Victor surprised me by not arguing. Instead, he nodded. "Yes, it is perfect. Esperanza. Our baby girl. Our baby vampire."

As Victor sat beside where I lay in my bed, I held one of Esperanza's tiny hands. Love flooded through me as I stared at her. Everything changed again, as it must. "Espy, my little Espy," I whispered.

During Espy's early months, Victor and I shared duties in taking care of her. There were cloth diapers to change and her feedings, although both tasks were much more enjoyable with her than a mortal human child. As Espy began to grow and exhibit signs of awareness of life around her, Victor tracked her progress, keeping his journal in Espy's nursery. He was always taking notes about her, remarking at just how extraordinary she was. After carefully explaining his ongoing work to me, I finally allowed him to take her into the laboratory, under my supervision, so that he could test her intelligence, agility and strength.

Espy was so much more than a baby. She possessed an intellect unlike human children of her age. She said her first word at three months: "mama." She pronounced "da-da" a week later. She began forming sentences by her first birthday. She was remarkable in every way.

Certainly, most parents believe their children are gifted, but Espy really was. She was special, the first child born of vampires by vampires.

Parenting seemed to suit both Victor and I, although he eventually returned to his studies after Espy's birth. Many of his studies now revolved around her, though, which meant that we spent more time together as a family than before she came into our lives.

For a short time, we were happy. My boredom soon fell away, thanks to the duties of motherhood. As Espy grew, I put myself in charge of tutoring her, teaching her those subjects that Urseline nuns and my mentors once taught to me in my formative years. By the age of four, Espy could name of all of the great art masters, and by eight, she was also well-versed in reading and mathematics. She grew up bilingual, with exposure to both French and German, but she also became adept at writing and speaking English, too.

She was a marvel, our little Espy, one that we took great pride in. But as her body grew older, so, too, did her appetites.

Espy was 12 years old when a group of villagers came to our castle, desperately seeking our help. Five children had gone missing from the village in less than a week. The townspeople were frantic, and imparted stories upon Victor and I about monsters that hid within the depths of the nearby forest. Victor was the lord of the property that made up the village, and therefore, it was his responsibility to find out what happened to those children, and if necessary, kill the monster.

I cringed as I stood within the castle's foyer listening to descriptions of a creature with three eyes that ate children and breathed fire, but kept my countenance blank. Victor appeared to listen raptly and nodded, as if he understood their concerns. "I will most certainly look into it," he announced with complete sincerity, although he quickly ushered the villagers out of our home. As the door closed behind them, he uttered, "Superstitious nonsense."

I smiled at his assessment in agreement.

"But I suppose I should make an effort," he sighed as he wrung his hands.

Espy came down the grand stairway and hugged her father. "Make an effort for what?" she asked.

I patted Espy's perfect little blonde head. "It's nothing, darling. Just some children missing from the village."

"Oh," Espy said as she looked up at me, her blue eyes wide and sparkling. "I can help with that."

Victor and I shared a glance at each other, our eyebrows raised.

"You can?" Victor asked, smirking at the precociousness of our daughter's offer.

Espy nodded and took both of our hands. "Come," she simply stated as she began pulling at us to follow. She led us through the main hall of the castle and out its back door, which led to the gardens.

"What is all this about, *ma fille*?" I inquired.

Espy said nothing as she pointed at a clump of rose bushes. Her left eye twitched uncontrollably as she stared straight ahead. She held her hands in front of her, clenched.

Victor quickly glanced at me, shrugged and then dropped Espy's hand to investigate further. As soon as he looked into the bushes, though, his face went pale. He brought a hand up to his mouth and shook his head.

Noting his behavior, I approached him, but stopped when he held a palm up and motioned for me to stay away.

I noticed hundreds of flies milling around the bushes just before the smell of decaying flesh assaulted my nostrils. A pile of small rotted bodies lay among the thorny branches, carelessly tossed there.

"I ate them," Espy said as she skipped over to where I stood, taking my hand once more.

I closed my eyes and swallowed hard. I reminded myself that she was just a child, and a vampire one at that. I forced myself to breathe deeply, calmly, as Victor stared at the bodies of the dead children.

"Espy, darling, we need to talk," I said as I began dragging her away from the scene and back to the castle. As we walked inside, I laid out the rules of our kind, explaining that we did not kill villagers and we certainly did not leave their bodies to rot in our garden. I made it clear that if she were ever hungry that she was to come to me or her father and let us know.

Espy listened intently and stared at the ground, her head hung in shame. "I'm sorry, Mother," she said, as tears began to drip down her cheeks.

"I know, darling, I know," I told her as I pulled her into a hug. But touching her felt dirty, somehow, and I, too, felt guilty.

Espy's tears soon dried and she looked up at me. There was

still an odd purity about her, in spite of what she had done. My disgust and guilt faded.

"My darling," I replied as I leaned over and kissed her on the forehead.

Victor soon joined us, dusting off his hands. Dirt was on his cheek, suggesting that he had buried the bodies. "We'll tell the village that it was wolves," he announced. "It was a pack of wolves and I took care of it."

Years passed without further incident. Happiness returned to our family, as seasons turned so quickly that it made them seem to blend into each other. Life was nothing more than Victor and Espy, but it was enough. Our daughter grew from a girl into a teenager, starting down the path that would her to becoming a young woman.

Espy always remained curious. She loved to ask questions. We never kept anything from her and we told her everything. She understood what she was and why she was different from the children in the village. She often asked me to regale her with tales of my life at Versailles, intrigued by my time among royalty. Once, she even asked me about the duties of a mistress. I answered every question as honestly as possible.

At times, Espy even seemed to model herself after me, even going so far as to wear my perfume, a vanilla and musk blend that was a gift to me from her father. Also like me, she understood the nature of sex early on. On her 16th birthday, we caught her in her room with a village boy, naked, the scent of lovemaking hanging in the air. Although I ran the boy off, I did not chide her because unlike human girls, she could not become pregnant from intimacies with mortals. And our morality was not the same as that of the time: we were a progressive family, one that did not find premarital sex immoral or wrong.

I did use the situation to instill a lesson to her, though: she needed to choose her toys more carefully. I followed that conversation with an invitation extended to several noble Austrian children to come stay with us occasionally at the castle. Once they began to arrive, Espy had her way with them, both boys and girls alike. But she never drank from them without our permission.

Bran Castle was a place without inhibitions, but it still had its rules, and that included my daughter. We were united in our intent, vampires who would never bring attention to that fact.

Espy often received letters at the castle, from far and wide, some from boys and girls she already had affairs with. Tales of her beauty expanded throughout the country, a beauty that was very much like my own. As she grew, we were often mistaken for sisters because we looked so much alike. She often received offers of marriage, but she, as we, denied them all. Espy did not have to marry or become a mistress because we raised her to become who she wished without the attachments that some women get forced to make to get ahead in a world ruled by men.

Espy had very few real friends, though and no companions that she really trusted. Instead, she turned to us, her family. She understood our vicarious situation as vampires, as well as the superstitions that people held against us. She understood the reasoning behind while our lifestyle remained a secret.

Espy's 18th birthday fast approached, and on the day, we organized a grand affair, a large party where we invited Austria's nobility to attend a grand soirée in our daughter's honor. I worked tirelessly with the staff, decorators and florists to have every detail just right. I spent many hours with Espy and the tailor to design the perfect dress for the event.

She made a grand entrance, albeit a fashionably late one, in that dress, featuring nothing but red silk and beads, a scandalous gown that amplified her cleavage and left her shoulders and arms completely bare. She was an enchantress in the gown, a seductress, all grown up and ready to take the world by storm. When she slowly made her way down the grand staircase in the castle's ballrooms, everyone went silent, staring at the beautiful young woman in red, their breaths caught in their throat.

It was like looking at myself through a mirror, reminding me vividly of my own grand entrance at Versailles, the night I captured the heart of a King.

Espy, though, did not need a King. Espy was just Espy, her own entity with her own mind, tied down to nothing or no one, save for us.

Epsy spent the evening gliding gracefully across the dance floor with multiple partners, again both men and women. As we watched her, Victor and I also danced, celebrating our beautiful immortal family. But at some point after a particularly enlivening waltz, Espy disappeared, and was gone for several hours.

This would not normally cause us concern, so we put off searching for her. She was a free soul and we did not put confines on her. If she wished to go elsewhere during her birthday party, she could. More than likely, she was somewhere private caught up in a moment of intimacy with one of her guests, perhaps several at a time.

After the orchestra's maestro expressed interest in playing a song especially written for our daughter, though, Victor and I excused ourselves from the gathering, and began searching the manor for Espy. She was not present in the house. We turned our search to the gardens, a place where Espy often liked to wander. We dashed through small mazes and rows of flowers, finally reaching the center plot of land, marked by a lone statue of Aphrodite. There, time slowed to a standstill.

We found a massacre strewn around the statue, which was now stained with blood. Piles of bodies lay around the goddess of love, their wrists cut, small pools of blood forming around their shapes.

My heart sank as I realized that there was still blood left in some of the bodies, although they had all experienced their last breath. This was not a normal vampire feeding. Instead it was mass murder.

Victor and I followed a trail of bloody footsteps through the back of the garden. These led to the rose gardens. Although the bushes were bare in November, their sweet floral scent still hung in the air. It was there where we found our daughter bent over a limp figure, a man she'd danced with earlier in the evening. Blood mingled with the red of her dress, her pale arms reaching up to the moonlight as she shook the man's body, screaming to the heavens, "Wake up!"

"Espy?" I whispered from where we stood staring at this horrific scene.

She looked up at me, her eyes wide, but clouded. "I couldn't get him to wake up. Why won't he wake up?" She dropped the body to the floor and brought her bloody hands in front of her face, as if seeing them for the first time.

"What have you done, child?" Victor asked sternly, in a voice rarely used with our child.

"She's killed… she's killed so many," I whispered to myself, as if morality had suddenly fallen upon me like a large stone. I attempted to comfort myself with the knowledge that this is what we do, as vampires, that we kill. How many had I killed to feed myself? But this newfound sense of rightness would simply not flee: this was different. This was worse. Espy killed these people for the sole sake of killing.

Despair gripped me as I began to question the meaning of my existence in the world.

It was as if the real world, the one that contained Versailles and my life before, perhaps a world that knew what I was before I did, suddenly came crashing down and struck me in the face.

I barely noticed when Espy stood up and turned around to run farther into the garden. I saw Victor rush after her, following her terrified screams. I stumbled off after the two, but my mind was a fog of morality. I became Eve in the garden of Eden, alone, and wishing that I had never spoken to the snake.

I was overcome with it all as we caught up to Espy, who we found collapsed in front of a statue of Poseidon near the goldfish pool. Victor picked her up, and while carrying her, called for servants, telling them that the party was over and that the guests must leave immediately. He made an excuse for both the blood and the bodies, weaving a story about a madman in the garden, intent upon killing our guests, as well as our daughter. Apparently, we saved her just in time.

As Victor carried my daughter off, she looked at me, one of her eyes twitching. There was a far-off look in her gaze, as if her thoughts were a million miles away.

The world blurred as I followed him into our house, uttering empty words to the departing guests. They seemed to accept Victor's story at face value and never once asked why our daughter had blood stains around her mouth.

Later, my thoughts muddled, I went through the motions of retiring for the evening, but a great melancholy settled over me. I would never sleep well again.

My daughter was a monster. Victor was a monster. I, too, was a monster.

CHAPTER ELEVEN

My failure as a mother hung over my head like a dark cloud. But it was my failure as a human being that rained down upon me, reminding me that in my selfishness and sense of superiority, I had brought this damaged child into the world to enact every wild impulse she possessed.

Espy was not a human child, though. She was the product of two vampires. She was more vampire than either myself or Victor combined: her mutation made her something else, something we could not truly understand. And she, this monster, existed because of us, because of me.

The morning after Espy's party saw many servants vacating the premises, fearful of the monster we unwittingly had unleashed on the world. This made the disposal of the bodies in the garden solely the responsibility of Victor and me. As Espy remained locked in her room, we quietly took to the task of dragging her victims through the garden, digging holes at the edge of the property and burying them. There were no words between us as we worked. Like me, the incident left Victor marred, but his occasional mumblings led me to believe that he only saw her as an experiment gone horribly wrong.

We had sent out word that the killer had been put to justice on our castle grounds, blaming it on a villager who had allowed superstition to get the best of him. Victor bribed some villagers to corroborate the story about this fictional man, and our public lives were spared.

We struggled with our private thoughts, mostly concerned about what to do with our daughter.

Espy stayed locked in her room quietly for several nights.

Victor and I spent those evenings in separate beds. By the third day, though, she began screaming unintelligible and random things that were not even words. More servants left in the chaos, eventually leaving our unhealthy little family as the only inhabitants of the castle.

Guilt held me in its grip and wrapped itself around my chest like fire. It burned away at my heart and left me hating everything about who I was and what I had allowed myself to become.

"It's the blood," Victor insisted as he began to obsess over his journals again and his studies in his laboratory. "Something is wrong with her blood."

I would only shrug at his words because now, I, like Espy, was a broken thing.

The castle fell into a state of disrepair. The wooden floors took on a dull sheen and began to crack. The stone walls lost their luster. A layer of dust settled on the furniture. Candle wax dripped onto the floor and solidified there, forever marking the chaos that controlled our lives. Cobwebs formed in the corners of every room, small spiders crawling through their nests without fear of being unsettled. The silver began to tarnish and golden embellishments turned green. Metal rusted and began to fall away. Windows broke and were left untended. Shattered glass, blood and dirt littered the floors. Tapestries began to fray. The colorful flags that hung from the turrets ripped away in storms: they were never replaced.

I lost track of time as life became an unbearable torment that I felt I deserved. I saw less of Victor as he locked himself in the basements, intent upon his scientific study of what went wrong with our daughter. He was so sure he could fix her, but I knew better. He took blood from her on those rare occasions that she was calm and studied it under microscopes until his eyes went blurry. He still dreamed of a world where vampires could exist, an evolved species that could teach humanity about the future.

When we were together, we often argued about Espy and what to do with her. It seemed cruel to keep her locked in her room, but what other solution did we have? Victor insisted that she would eventually normalize, but I had my doubts. It was I, in the end, who was right: Espy seemed to grow more insane as months passed, followed by years.

We kept her alive, though, although we could no longer trust her to feed herself. I took over the duties of finding her victims myself, as a sort of penance, but I changed the types of people I brought to her. I chose only those who rode on the lowest rungs of society: thieves, murderers and rapists. I used the opportunity for myself and Espy to become a swift justice for those who would dare do others wrong. This was a new promise I made to myself in my guilt: I would only take the lives of those who truly deserved to die.

Espy's feeding rituals, though, still terrified me. She ripped through her victims' necks with her fingernails, but did not just stop at drinking their blood. She also ate their flesh, becoming a cannibal, something that made me no longer recognize my daughter. I made myself watch her, though, and I disposed of the unrecognizable sacks of flesh she left behind in her wake. On those occasions when she allowed me to touch her, I cleaned her up, understanding that this was all part of my punishment.

Guilt is a nasty thing and ate away at me as surely as Espy ate away at her victims. I became despondent and sank into a depression that left me feeling unwhole, unclean and undeserving.

I once attempted suicide. Although we were immortal, we could die, but I soon learned that death was harder to achieve for those of our kind. That knowledge still did not stop me from hanging a rope in my bedchamber from my chandelier as I carefully stood on a chair with a noose around my neck. I kicked the chair away and strangled, grateful when I felt the world grow gray and dark. I thought death overcame me, but in the end, I hung there for a few hours and woke up from the noise when the rope snapped and my body crashed to the floor.

I tried overdosing on Victor's sleeping draughts, but only woke up after with a severe headache and an unsettled stomach. I knew what I was, so perhaps I was only going through empty motions in trying to kill myself. My body was stronger than a human's and had a greater capacity for healing, all thanks to the mutation that made me a vampire. Dying soon seemed more impossible than difficult, although Victor once told me that ripping our hearts out of our chests or having our bodies burned to cinders might do the trick. But we had never tried that, so who's to say we would not return in some sort of misshapen form, even from such mutilations?

Eventually, Victor's research took over his life. He became obsessed, and with that obsession came madness. As each year progressed, I saw less of him. I was not even sure if he was even still alive down there in the oppressing darkness of the dungeons after he didn't bother to come up for months. He moved Espy down there with him, leaving me alone in the cold and empty chateau.

Loneliness is a gray companion who stays with you when all others fail. But there came a time when I could no longer face it, nor live another day under that roof. I had only one option available to me: I needed to leave Bran Castle and go back out into the world.

I packed up my things in trunks and suitcases and wrote a note for Victor:

"My dearest Victor, my amour. I fear that I cannot spend one more moment here at Bran Castle. If I do not leave, I will become as mad as our daughter. It is time for me to go out into the world once more. I do hope that you will forgive me, Cherie. I promise that you and our beloved Espy will always remain in my heart. May you both remain safe. Forever Yours, Reinette."

I briefly thought of slipping the letter under the basement door, but I did not wish to get that close to Victor ever again, for fear I would lose my resolve and stay. Instead, I slipped it into the corner of the frame of a painting of Espy that we commissioned on her 14th birthday, the one that hung in the foyer above a dusty old table.

Certainly, I felt some guilt at leaving, but not as much as I might have thought I should experience. There was nothing left that I could do for Victor or Espy.

I tried to imagine Victor reading the letter and falling to his knees in tears, and yet, I knew that this was an empty promise of my imagination. He would no more grieve for me than he did for the servants who abandoned the castle during the first days of Espy's madness. Our affair was over.

Perhaps, in leaving, I was a coward, but I pledged to do better in the next lifetime. Because this was just the end of one life, much like my death scene at Versailles. I was like the mythical phoenix: after I burned the ashes of this Reinette, lover of Victor and mother of Espy, a new Reinette would emerge from the fire.

A horse-drawn carriage carried me away from Bran Castle by moonlight, leaving behind Victor, Espy and Austria, and I made my way back to my beloved France.

CHAPTER TWELVE

Returning to France was not as easy as I thought. I traveled by carriage, with winter all around me. Heavy snowfall stopped my journey for several days in Strasbourg, where I began to hear rumors circulating of unrest, particularly in Paris. It seemed that the poorest citizens had now risen up in record numbers against the nobility, with many of the city's finest families finding themselves in prison, or worst, losing their heads to the blade of a guillotine.

France was no longer as I remembered it. It was beginning to become something else.

At first, I assumed these tales were just here say, stories made up by bored villagers to pass the long cold days of the season. But once I was on the road again, I began to see the first signs of revolution, especially outside Paris. There were crudely constructed wooden signs along the road with the slogan "Liberté, égalité, fraternité." As I reached the outskirts of the city and entered the 11th arrondissement, my carriage met with a group of angry peasants waving torches and swords, screaming the words "Le revolution!"

Gendarmes attempted to push the protesters away from the road, but their efforts fueled the crowd's anger and a fight broke out. In the chaos, my carriage toppled over, spilling me out into the street with the wreckage, a former noblewoman dressed in fine men's clothes. As someone put a torch to the carriage, a pair of hands grabbed me from beneath my armpits and dragged me away to a safe distance.

Out of breath, I squinted through the smoke to look at my rescuer. She was an olive-skinned woman with bright blue eyes, the kind of eyes that could reach into the depths of my secrets. Her hair was short, cut like a man's, but with ragged edges, as if she had cut it hastily, perhaps in an act of rebellion. Her clothing was like mine: men's breeches with a long coat. She also wore long leather boots that went over her knees. Even in the wintry and smoky air, I caught the scent of vanilla wafting from her.

"Mademoiselle? Are you hurt?" she asked as she pulled my head into her lap. One small, but rough, hand caressed my face, pushing hair out of my eyes.

Flames blazed around us and smoke rose lazily into the air. Men and women yelled and cursed at each other, screaming and crying.

And yet, in this woman's arms, I felt safe from the violence.

I nodded, still dazed by this sudden turn of events. My mind tried to wrap itself around this revolution that I found myself in the middle of. Paris was burning, and yet, somehow it felt appropriate, in line with the burning within my soul. Fire could cleanse and make things clean, could it not? As a woman formerly tied to the nobility and forced to become a mistress to gain status, this new chaos somehow inspired me. It represented something I very much needed: change.

I turned my head to watch as a group of men and women organized into a line across the road and linked arms. They marched down the street singing "La Marseillaise." I suddenly wanted nothing more than to march with them, to become a part of what was happening here. Perhaps I saw a chance at redemption, a way to give back to a society that I had taken so much from.

I sat up and took the woman's hand, as if afraid that she were not real, merely a mirage. "I want to help," I said, meeting her gaze.

The woman squeezed my hand and quietly nodded. "I am Marceline," she said.

I smiled, my eyes never leaving her face. "Reinette," I answered, feeling a strange sense of peace washing over me, despite the cacophony of sound around us.

She stood up and helped me to my feet. "Welcome to the revolution, Reinette."

Marceline took me to the rebellion's headquarters, a little ramshackle building of separate apartments in Paris. I informed her that I was just recently returning to Paris from abroad and that I wanted to become part of the revolution that gripped the country. I began decrying those "masters of torment," that wealthy citizenship I was once a member of. I said pretty words about how I hated the nobility and how they only oppressed me and the people.

Although I once loved luxury, once I said these words, I realized that I actually meant them. And as I began to believe in the cause, I felt hope for the first time since leaving Austria and Bran Castle. Something important was happening in the country of my birth, and it was something I was now a part of.

In overthrowing the nobility and the royalty, France would become something more, something where women, and the poor, regardless of birth, would have equality. It was a naive thought, but after all my suffering, I needed to believe that I could change the world for the better.

Marceline and I became closer with each passing day as we worked in the trenches of the revolution. We often talked about the future life we hoped to make in France. I felt a kinship with her and admired her for her willingness to risk her life for the things she believed in. I wanted to become like her, and through that, I found meaning in life once more.

Much of what happened in the country, though, was also partly my fault. France never recovered the from decisions I had made as mistress, not even after King Louis XV's death. The Treaty of Versailles that I pushed for had laid the groundwork that gave the peasants the need to rebel. It even served as a spark for the American Revolutionary War. But there was good mixed in with the bad: the world seemed ready to break from the chains of monarchy and create something where all were more equal.

As the revolution took Paris in a stranglehold, I watched noble families fall. I saw Bastille become a prison for many of them, all charged with crimes against France. I watched Marie Antoinette, and others, lose their heads to the guillotine.

I drank my fill of noble blood in those days, telling myself that they were criminals and that this was my way in helping the cause. So many of those held in the Bastille ended up dead, drained of blood. No one questioned my visitations of some of those held there, nor did they question bodies turning up bloodless. I fed without fear or guilt, telling myself I was doing my part in making the world better by ridding it of these vile creatures.

Yes, the revolution was a distraction from my old life, but it also gave me something else: hope.

It was Marceline, though, that gave me more. Friends were not something I ever had many of. Perhaps it was because we were fighting in the trenches in close quarters, but Marceline and I became quick companions.

But it was after one specific drunken celebration where our group touted our grand deeds against the bourgeois when I realized that I loved her. The wine flowed freely that evening and I drank much of it myself. My mutation rarely allows me the luxury of getting drunk, but everyone else around me was highly inebriated. This included Marceline, who spent the evening dancing on tables and singing songs about victory and justice. Once she tired, though, she settled beside me in a wooden chair in a dirty Parisian bar that was a local revolutionary haunt.

"Reine," she said. "No matter what happens tomorrow, please know that I love you." She then leaned in, and before I realized it, kissed me on the lips. This was not a simple kiss of friendship, though, but something more, something previously left unsaid.

I responded to the softness of her mouth, the delicate way her lips graced their way past mine and ran a hand through her dirty brown hair. I had never kissed a woman before, but I found the experience more than pleasant: it was positively exhilarating.

Her words, though, came back to disturb me once the kiss was over. No matter what happens tomorrow? What did that mean? Before I had a chance to ask, Marceline bounced away, jumping on the table again to give a rousing rendition of "The Carmagnole."

I began to listen to the whispers around me and soon learned that the rebellion had plans to infiltrate a meeting of those close to the royal family with hopes of capturing some of the highest nobles in the country. Those nobles would go to the Bastille, to justice, to the guillotine. Serving as one of the leaders of the attack was Marceline.

A pit formed in my stomach as I learned of this. I pulled her off the table and into my arms, pleading with her not to go. "You must stay here," I begged, my hands wrapped around her waist. "With me."

Marceline shook her head and extricated herself from my embrace, "Oh, Reine, have faith," she said as she raised a glass. "God is on our side. God favors the disenfranchised." She took a big swig from her ale and kissed me again.

I began to lose track of time. Marceline grabbed me into a dance, becoming bolder with every sip she took. Before the night was over, we found ourselves tangled up in sheets in a small room upstairs, our hands exploring each others' bodies. It was a night of pleasure unlike anything I ever knew as our soft bodies molded together, our hips undulating in primal rhythms beneath fingertips and tongues.

My body spent itself again and again and I found a brief happiness that washed over me like the sun on a new day. Austria was all but forgotten, my murderous child quickly dismissed as a figment of my imagination. I had purpose and I had love. I was reborn anew, the phoenix risen from the flames.

When I woke in the morning, though, Marceline was gone.

The cycle of love, life and death is often an abrupt thing, and especially so in war. Marceline's mission failed and she died. I did not see her again until they brought her burnt and nearly unrecognizable body back to the pub several days later. We had a small ceremony there, for her and several others who perished. I did not even think to mourn. Instead, I devoted myself to making Marceline's vision for the world to come to fruition.

I modeled myself after her and began organizing marches and protests throughout Paris. This was despite the increasing violence spreading throughout the city, with the revolution soon taking a nasty turn, ushering in the Reign of Terror.

Even after destroying the monarchy and most of the city's nobility, the poor remained poor and the wealthy - at least those who remained - stayed wealthy. Frustration grew among those who sought equality and fairness. Although France changed during the revolution, it also stayed the same, much to the chagrin of those counting on the revolution to change things.

A committee ruled the city with an iron fist. And although that committee claimed to side itself with the people, those people who got out of line or spoke out against it were often killed. Dissension was discouraged, although it was the very thing to cause the revolution in the first place. The revolution became chaos and Paris became a city only friendly to those in power.

France was a republic, with a constitution, but its people still suffered at the hands of those who ruled them.

Nothing had changed. But I continued to fight for those things I believed were right, for those things Marceline had taught me.

Those who were once the voice of the people soon became criminals. I watched many of my revolutionary friends marched to the Bastille. And yet, I continued to speak out for justice, more empowered than ever.

Women, in particular, often saw their deaths at the blade of the guillotine. The last group executed during the revolution were all women, including several nuns, women who refused to give up their religious vows. I never understood religion, nor partook in it, but this act of tyranny opened my eyes, as well as the eyes of other. The violence had to end.

At the head of it all was a man named Robespierre, but as often happens when people rise up to grasp power when a country is vulnerable, he soon fell, thanks to efforts from groups of rebels like my own. We stormed into the Hall of Paris and demanded justice, sending him to his end. His blood was some of the last that stained the steps of the Bastille.

Although the revolution ended, my path to redemption was still new. I embraced a new kind of freedom, one that came with responsibility. I now understood the difference between right and wrong. I began questioning the morality of every decision I made. When thoughts of Victor and Espy arose, I forced them away, letting them sit inside my mind like an old dream long forgotten. I was more now, I was better, I was someone doing something for people other than myself.

Once things settled down in France, though, I realized that some things never change. I was, after all, still a woman, and even with the new regime, my voice still counted for little. But for a while, we mattered, but then we returned back to becoming wives, mothers and mistresses.

And my beloved country still belonged to men.

CHAPTER THIRTEEN

There was a short time after the revolution, though, that gave revel and pride to the women who took part in it. And among the peasants, women were almost seen as equals, but as is always the case, men are still the ones who rise to power and take it away from those who are not like them.

And this is how Napoleon Bonaparte rose through the ranks of the military to become the leader of France. He was a small and ugly little man, with an uglier mind, intent not on just the domination of France, but of the world. He was mad, as is often the case with egomaniacs, sneaking his way into power by taking advantage of how lax people became after the revolution. We thought the revolution saved us, but instead, it did nothing more but hand France over to men like him.

At first, Napoleon was just the great champion for France, but as he became more touted, especially in the media that he owned, his influence on the country became greater. After a series of successful battles elsewhere in the world, including Italy, the people cheered him on as a national hero.

I never trusted a man so ambitious, so I never trusted Napoleon to do what was best for France. I sneered upon seeing newspaper articles about his greatness, all with portraits of him that made him seem far greater in stature than he really was. The people cheered for him and waved flags in his presence as if he were the second coming of Christ. Before too long, he took that adoration to work his way up to becoming the head of France.

The revolution liberated France and handed her to a dictator. Under Napoleonic rule, the old system began reasserting itself.

Although the nobility and feudal systems were gone, the equality we fought for never appeared. Instead, we held up soldiers and armies as nobility, full of men, with the only positions for women at home in the tending of washing, cleaning and raising children.

All that work for naught: France fell into its old ways. And yet the French people continued to cheer for this insecure deplorable man. I knew that he would become our downfall and once more, France would face a turning point.

I took to navigating various social circles. I spent my days with the peasants, those who I fought with during the revolution. I spent my evenings at palaces and balls, where I became Reinette Leclair, a distant cousin of Madame de Pompadour. My faux character's history was untraceable, but I knew enough about my own life that I could act convincingly enough. I also used this lie to explain my resemblance to the portraits of me that still hung in great halls, which also helped me gain entrance into the social gatherings of the wealthy. These parties were no longer enjoyable for me, though, tainted by the blood spilled during the revolution, tainted by memories of Marceline.

But I was on a mission: to understand what was happening with the rise of Napoleon, someone who did not have France's best interests in mind. I wanted to know why my people so readily handed the country over to him. So I worked my way through these parties until I finally received an invitation to a ball that would feature his presence to celebrate his claim as Emperor of France.

The party was at the Palais de Tuileries, Napoleon's official residence in the city. I dressed for the occasion in a deep violet gown tailored to accent my best features: my long neck, my porcelain skin, my ample breasts and my blue eyes. I no longer enjoyed wearing clothes as this, much preferring my man's clothes, but my usual attire was hardly appropriate for such a grand affair. Society forced me to once more take on the duties of what it expected of women, whether I liked it or not. But I did plan on taking my women's clothing and charms and using it to my advantage.

I waited in line with other wealthy members of the French

public, each taking a few minutes to acknowledge the Emperor who sat on a throne-like chair at the far end of the room. One by one, they each bowed to him, as if he were a king - which he was not. I placed myself at the end of the line to make the best impression, and when my turn came due, I was the only one standing in front of the man. I used my grace to bow deftly to him, my head held up so that I could catch his gaze. As expected, he only stared at my breasts.

Men are all the same, I thought with disgust, although the smile on my face held no indication of thoughts other than curiosity and openness.

"Madame," Napoleon said in a puny voice. "You do me an honor by offering up such beauty to these dull surroundings." He motioned around himself with a short arm, the fingers on his hand all seeming like thumbs.

"Thank you," I answered demurely, rising and placing my hands in front of me, against the expensive fabric of my dress. I blinked several times, letting my eyelashes send a message of nothing more than kindness and ignorance.

Napoleon stood up, although at his full height, he was still a few inches shorter than me. I looked down at him, trying not to laugh at the man who saw himself as Paris' new king, even though he refused to call himself that. It was also common knowledge that he once executed a man who made fun of his lack of stature. Perhaps that is why he felt it necessary to conquer the world: to make up for something he lacked.

"So, you are related to the infamous Madame de Pompadour?" he asked as he took my hand.

His hand was cold and felt clammy, even through my gloves. It took a strong will to not drop it immediately. As he drew closer, I smelled a dirty musk scent surrounding him, as if he rarely bathed or even invested in perfumes. But I continued to smile to hide my disdain, not indicating that I did not like him, nor did I respect him.

"Yes," I answered, lowering my head in deference. "But only distantly."

He nodded, continuing to hold my hand against my will. "I would argue that you are even more beautiful than she," he remarked. His voice attempted gallantry, but failed. Instead, his words felt insincere and disturbing.

I would need a long hot bath before this evening ended.

I maintained my posture, though, even as his hand clung to mine. He pulled himself closer. I said nothing as he breathed in deeply, as if noting my scent. It felt like he was attempting to steal my soul. I felt violated.

Someone stood behind me, waiting in line to meet the Emperor. I took that as my excuse to leave. "I'm afraid I've taken up enough of your time," I said as I forcefully pulled my hand away and gestured to the gentleman behind me.

Napoleon seemed annoyed at the intrusion, but nodded nonetheless. Duty called and someone else wanted to dole adoration upon him. "Yes, well, perhaps you could save me a dance for later in this evening?" he asked, his eyebrows raised. He looked ridiculous.

I nodded, with no intent of keeping any such promise. I quickly moved out of the way and through the room, pulling off the gloves I'd been wearing and tossing them to the ground just before I jumped into my carriage.

All my instincts were right about the man. He was greedy with power and never happy with what he accomplished. He always wanted more. So he tried for more, until it consumed him. His lust for power nearly destroyed France, but we had Britain to thank in finally defeating him into submission at Waterloo. By then, the country began questioning Napoleon's motives, as well as the direction he had in mind for France. There was more debt, thanks to all the wars, and we became the country that no one wanted to ally with. By the time Napoleon returned to Paris, a defeated man, he was highly unpopular. This led to his eventual exile.

But he left damage in his wake. France returned to its monarchy and put Louis XVIII on the throne. France forgot about the revolution and its people. Royalty and nobility ruled again. I felt betrayed, as if everything I once fought for was lost.

Those I fought with forgot, too, so glad were they to see Napoleon displaced. Even the women who once stood beside me demanding equality quieted, going back to their lives as daughters, mothers and wives. I soon learned that history had a nasty way of repeating itself. The only consistency is that kingdoms rise and fall. This is as true today as it was then. Even now, women remain invisible in a world run by men.

But I became a woman who would never let a man take what was mine. And if anything, France was mine. I continued to offer my voice to those who would hear it and I hung in philosophical circles that questioned the status quo. I remained a mouthpiece for the disenfranchised.

Eventually, things did change for the better because of people like me. France became a constitutional monarchy, meaning that the new King held less power than those who came before. Progress continued and Louis XVIII was the last monarch to ever rule France.

My country began to flourish in its newfound freedom. I took time for myself to rest, to read and to continue feeding upon the evildoers of the world. The 1800s brought France to enlightenment, leading up to the World's Fair in 1889 that saw the construction of one of the greatest architectural structures in the world, the Eiffel Tower. I watched its progress as the modern world invaded my city. While others complained about its ugliness and its horrible contemporary appeal, I embraced its beauty, understanding that it was a symbol for the things France struggled for and gained. Marceline would have loved it.

CHAPTER FOURTEEN

The world moved on, as did I. I continued rallying against the establishment. I was an outspoken activist and feminist, making my voice known against those powers that would suppress women. I marched with suffragettes. I gave speeches against war. I fought the patriarchy. I worked tirelessly with efforts that aligned with those things I so desperately now believed in.

I was no longer Madame de Pompadour, that self-suffering elitist noble that once wandered the halls of Versailles. I was Reinette, a force of nature that was of the people and for the people. Long gone was the little girl who once dreamed of becoming mistress to a king.

I was also a vampire, one who fed from evildoers, mostly those men who preyed upon women and children. I was a lover, seeking comfort in the arms of both men and women, any who would open their heart to me, if only for an evening. I shunned romantic love, though, thinking there was too much work to do to focus on such things as the world cycled through change.

Dictators rose and fell. Countries appeared and disappeared. Men fought for power. Women fought for equality. The Earth spun on its axis, forever moving in circles.

An assassination brought about a new war, one more convoluted than the wars that came before it. Its cause remained murky with no one truly understanding that there is a fine line between right and wrong. But this war brought German forces to France and my beloved country became a sea of trenches, blasts, bombs and death.

The men of France fought, while the women stayed behind

to pick up the slack. We took up jobs at farms and factories. We took over as heads of our families. Some of us wrote poems and letters to the men on the front, assuring them that things back home were fine.

Some of us took up nursing, tending to the wounded as they fell on the fields, bloody, battered and beaten.

While men fought each other, women ran the country and prevailed through the war. After, though, men met our loyalty with skepticism: once men returned to the farms and factories to reclaim what they thought was theirs, women were once more shoved to the sidelines, urged to do nothing more than make babies and dinner. Those women fortunate enough to continue on in actual jobs received less pay and poorer treatment than their male counterparts. Once more, men made the decisions that affected us all. We held no voice, we had no vote, we had no say in the goings-on of our country.

There was peace, but the cost was high. But as men are, in fact, men, war would soon arrive in France yet again.

Between the two world wars, I traveled throughout Europe, and settled briefly in Munich, a city that suited me with its old-fashioned ways. There, the people still wore their traditional garb, men flaunting their legs in lederhosen and women dancing in their colorful dirndls as the sound of polka music filled the air. It was a city out of time and place, even with the emergence of insanity that would soon grip other German cities. Munich seemed as far apart from the world of war as one could get.

I found Munich unique and charming. Every day at noon, the Rathaus-Glockenspiel, an elaborate clock, would entertain passers-by with stories told with dolls and bells rotating at its uppermost towers. The city was almost like something out of a fairy tale, and there was even a stone dragon climbing its way up the city's town hall.

The people from Munich intrigued me. They were friendly, even to a stranger with a French accent. I often received invitations to private homes for dancing, drinking and beer, all things I did not need to survive, but that I still sometimes liked to partake in such affairs because of the sense of community that these gatherings brought. The city's beer halls always teemed with life, laughter and song, and often made me forget my sorrows.

I used my time in Munich to regain my senses as time marched on. I indulged in new skills, learning my way around swords by taking fencing lessons. I even took up ballet, finding that my body still handled dance with ease. Everything I learned helped me find more of myself, the strength that lay inside.

Munich's warmth enveloped me as I walked down its streets admiring its pointed towers and turrets, buildings dedicated to a saint who once fought a mythical dragon. I sat in restaurants without ordering just to enjoy the odors of beer and apple strudel wafting through the air.

But all good things end, and eventually, Munich began to change. A hateful spirit began spreading throughout Germany, even into my new adopted home. The Nazis took control of government, with the intention of ruling all of it, including Bavaria. That hatefulness began to leak into the city's daily life, even as news came in of internment camps and bombs getting dropped on top of London.

The age of Adolph Hitler arrived. But it was the people who followed the man that were far more terrifying. Although some had no choice in the matter, most elected to put him in power simply because they liked the way he spoke. He was not a politician, they said, but a man of the people. He said the things that many Germans thought, but feared to say aloud. Yes, his ideas were extreme, but the Nazis believed the world was in turmoil and that required extreme measures.

Hitler rose to power on the backs of the people who supported him and so the second World War was as much a fault of theirs as it was his. Those who truly believed in the Nazi way, those anti-Semites who truly believed Hitler's words, were now everywhere. Once, they had hidden in shadows, but when Hitler came to power, they embraced daylight and became the most powerful force in the world.

They hated Jews simply for being Jews. Interment camps popped up all over the country where Jews were experimented on, put to hard labor, beaten and gassed to death all because they did not have the blonde hair and blue eyes of the "pure" Germans. And although it seemed that the Nazis appeared over night, they were the result of a fear and hatred that had been breeding for hundreds of years.

The Nazis spread across Europe like a plague, conquering anyone who would dare say anything against them. They censored the press and advocated news that only supported their theories. They shut up critics by killing them. They terrorized cities and took over property and homes, stating that it was their right. And the farther their power spread, the more Nazis that came out of the woodwork. Freedom died with the rise of Hitler, killed by those who followed him and those who refused to fight him.

My time in Munich came to an end as news arrived that the Nazis planned on marching into Paris, my home. I fled Germany in secrecy, sneaking across borders to return to my homeland, my France. I would not let her suffer at the hands of the enemy.

How strange to think that I, a vampire and monster, would live to see an evil far greater than any I ever posed. I arrived in France with one intent: to drink the blood of Nazis and to fight. Fighting came easy for me, and it helped that I spoke both French and German. I set myself up as a performer in a cabaret, using my beauty, as well as my talent for singing and dancing, to lure Nazis into my dressing room to meet their deaths at the blade of my little knife. I became a serial murderer, but no one ever suspected the innocent-faced cabaret performer who sang with the voice of an angel. I planned on taking down every Nazi one by one, all while assuring that my belly stayed full.

But fate had something more important in mind. And soon, those who would seek to remove the Nazis from Paris approached me, asking me to indulge in work that was far more dangerous, yet also more intriguing.

In 1944, I became a spy for the French resistance.

CHAPTER FIFTEEN

The French resistance chose me not just for my beauty, but also for my physical prowess and the easy way I spoke both French and German. I already knew how to work with knives and swords, and I was a quick study with guns, too. I learned about the delicate intrigues of spy work, and my position in the cabaret gave me the perfect opportunity to learn the enemy's secrets.

The cabaret was often a meeting place for German soldiers, including those higher in command. As Ada Lang, I performed both onstage and off, using my talent and low-cut sequined dresses to woo even the hardest of hearts. It was the role of a lifetime, and far more important than anything I'd ever done. My work could decide the fate of France.

The Nazis were everywhere in Paris, installed within the city's streets and buildings. Even the Eiffel Tower belonged to them. Any French man or woman who spoke out against their presence often found themselves dead and bloated, floating in the Seine.

It was a dangerous time, but I sang my heart out and whispered false words into the ears of those who had information to share. And I passed that information on to the resistance, in hopes that each detail would bring Paris closer to liberation.

Eventually, the German commanders requested special audiences just with me. I refused, at first, playing the coquette, all part of the plan. This made them want me even more, and they never took "no" for an answer. The Nazis, especially, seemed to enjoy being refused, loving to demand that women bow to their every will. I would, but only because I chose to.

One of those commanders was General Dietrich von Choltitz, the man Hitler put in charge of the entire city. I played my part when he requested a private meeting with me after one of my shows.

I finished my set with a resounding chorus of "Lili Marlene," a favorite of the German soldiers. I took my bows and exited stage right, quickly rushing to my dressing room where the general would meet me. I stripped out of my long black gown and slipped into a simple satin robe, left open enough to leave little to the imagination. One shoulder of the robe was hanging off my shoulder, seemingly by accident, showing skin that I hoped the man would long to touch.

The General arrived shortly after my performance with a bouquet of roses, all yellow, my least favorite color. But I took them graciously and doted on them, thanking him immensely for his kindness before placing them into a vase that sat on my dressing table. I batted my eyelashes and posed, making myself docile in his eyes, all the while hiding the deep-rooted hatred I held in my heart for he and his kind.

I danced through the room and sat down on a chaise lounge, gesturing for him to join me there. The robe slipped up to show most of my legs, which I crossed delicately at the ankles.

He sat beside me, close enough that his uniformed leg brushed against mine. He wrapped an arm around the back of the sofa, his fingertips gracing my bare shoulder. I trembled in disgust, but hid it as a sign of passion.

He never saw through my guise. I marveled at the stupidity of men who thought they were superior to everyone else.

I placed a hand on his knee and pulled myself closer, allowing the robe to slip down and uncover more of my bosom.

I felt his pulse begin to race with desire as he reacted to my advances. He leaned in to kiss me, tasting of tobacco and gin. While his tongue traced circles around mine, his hand deftly freed me of the robe and then moved down across my body to find purchase between my legs. He began rubbing me there, rough. Taking, not asking.

But I let him because this was what I did. And I knew that in letting him have his way with me, I would have my way with him later and learn everything I needed to about the Nazis' plans for the city. I did it for France.

Perhaps that made me a whore, but I was a whore who would save her beloved country.

When he pushed me down on the chaise lounge and undid his pants, I did not struggle. Instead, I made little moaning gasps to make him think that I wanted this. I continued to make those noises as he entered me and expended himself quickly.

During his climax, our eyes met and I knew that he was mine.

"Herr von Choltitz," I said with a perfect German accent. I cooed and purred in his ear.

"General," he corrected me as he roughly tugged on my long blonde hair.

"Forgive me, general," I said, still playing coy, my words barely a murmur. "Thank for taking the time to spend with me. That was..." I struggled with words, with the lie, but played it off. "Most entertaining." I laughed, because it seemed appropriate, a light little thing, something that sounded joyful, but was actually sarcastic. I derived no pleasure from this man.

"Yes, it was," he announced as he rolled over and lay beside me, his pants still undone. He wrapped one arm around my naked body, as if claiming me as his own.

"We should do this again, "I said, not really meaning it, but knowing that I would easily reel him in and learn his secrets.

He nodded.

There was a knock on the door, followed by a Nazi soldier barging into the room. The man came to attention and offered the general a salute, averting his eyes as the general buttoned up his pants and tossed my robe over me to cover my naked form. He glared at the soldier for the interruption, but kept his arm around me, showing off what he believed as his possession.

"I was instructed to inform you that it is time," the soldier stated as he stared straight ahead as if not noticing our state of undress.

"Leave me," the general instructed, offering a hasty salute from where he sat. "I will be there shortly."

"Go," I cooed, reaching up and tracing a delicate design on

his shoulder with my fingertips. "You have work to do. But I do hope you'll come again."

He stood up, straightened his uniform and left.

I saw him again the next night, and the night after that and the one after that for a week. He would make love to me in exactly the same way each time, never deviating from his routine. But I soon became certain that he was becoming enamored of me from the hurried way he always undressed me to the smile he offered after each encounter. He thought that he owned me, but I understood that it was the other way around. I had him.

Another week passed and we took to drinking and dining together before our lovemaking sessions. I began asking him little questions about his life and his background, followed by questions that let him regale me with the important nature of his job. He bragged about the virtues of the Nazi party, but he also started sharing small details of plans, things that would affect the war.

This is how I learned about the bombs that would destroy Paris. He told me that there were explosives planted all over the city. He only awaited the order from Hitler that would blow my home to pieces.

Later, I told the resistance about these plans, but time was of the essence and we still did not know where the Nazis had planted these bombs.

I had to do better. So I took it upon myself to save Paris.

One evening, after our lovemaking that left us breathless on the floor of my dressing room, General von Choltitz told me that the order to destroy Paris would soon come. He was on standby waiting for word from Hitler: once that order arrived, Paris would become nothing more than rubble and dirt. As he spoke, though, I heard something I could exploit: a hint of regret that suggested he actually had a better nature.

"But this city is so beautiful, don't you think?" I asked, frowning as he spoke of its impending destruction. "Don't you think it could become the beauty of the Nazi empire?" It would be such a shame to destroy it. To destroy this." I motioned around me, indicating not just the room in which we lay, but myself.

"You will be safe, I promise that," he stated.

"I cannot leave," I announced, sitting up, a worried expression on my face. "I love it here. This city took me in after my grief." I referred to a story I told him about how my family had died promoting the Nazi cause in Berlin. "She is my home now. Couldn't we make her part of the greater Germany?"

He looked around the room and then his eyes settled to gaze out the small window that overlooked an alley. He frowned. "It is a beautiful city," he admitted. "She is a beautiful mistress." He turned his attention to me, his words holding a double meaning.

I continued to play upon his doubt. "For me? Please? Can't we keep Paris?"

The general nodded and then shook his head, conflicted.

We both knew such an order would arrive soon. The allies were on their way and Hitler would rather burn the city to the ground that leave it standing for its liberation. I could not let that happen.

The general did not make a decision that night, but he was with me when the order to set Paris on fire finally arrived. Again, a soldier interrupted us, with a message trapped inside an envelope, a wax seal indicating that it was from Hitler himself. As the general opened and read the note, his expression told me everything I needed to know about its contents it was the order to detonate the bombs.

The general dropped the note to the floor and stared at me. I stared back, a single dramatic tear slipping down my cheek. Terror built up within me, a panic that I hid well, afraid that I had misjudged the situation.

He leaned down and picked up the piece of paper and tossed it into the fireplace, watching it turn to ash. "Paris is safe," he whispered as he stared at the fire.

And it was.

CHAPTER SIXTEEN

The day the allies rolled into Paris was one of the happiest the city could ever remember. France's citizens crowded the sidewalks and waved small French flags while they sang songs of French patriotism as allied tanks drove down the length of the Champs-Elysees.

The war was finally over.

Like other Parisians, I took to the streets, dancing and singing with others, complete strangers to me, but friends because we were all French and overjoyed that the long night of the Nazis had finally given in to day. The sun rose once more over Paris. The celebrations lasted into the night and the next day, continuing for nearly a week. During that time, no one slept: joy kept us awake because Paris was ours once again.

Not all Germans left the city, though. Small pockets of Nazis remained behind, spies convinced that the war wasn't over, that Hitler still lived and that their cause was still just. It was one of these men that nearly brought my end.

I danced in the streets for the fourth night in a row, my heart light, the smile of victory permanently placed on my lips in bright red lipstick. A man approached me, presumably a fellow French citizen who wanted to join the celebration. I held a hand out to him and spun myself in a circle, laughing.

But then I recognized him: he was one of the Nazi soldiers in service to the General I betrayed. I struggled to remember his name as he reached into his jacket and pulled out a pistol, pointing it at me with a grimace of hate. The gun fired and a hot blast of fire pierced my lower chest. The world began to slow as seconds became minutes. I felt the bullet enter my ribcage, just beneath my heart. Blood, that substance that sustained me, gushed from the wound left in the bullet's wake, staining my white dress as it splashed to the concrete beneath my feet. I stumbled back and fell. My eyes fixed on a star-filled sky that had only moments before held such promise. My breath grew ragged. Confusion and panic raced through my addled mind. The world blurred and began to fade.

I heard several women scream and the sound of hurried footsteps. There was a voice in my ear, a man's, that called out to me. "Mademoiselle?"

I felt a strange hand press itself against my forehead. It was warm against my chilled skin. Then it, and the world, went away, and everything drowned in black.

I woke up in a hospital. A sharp pain welcomed me as my consciousness returned. I was also hungry, hungrier than I had ever felt since my faked death at Versailles. Harsh lights greeted me as I opened my eyes, nearly blinding me, but I soon made out the shape of a nurse in a white dress standing over me.

"You have lost a lot of blood, *mademoiselle*," she stated, as she worked with a red bag of fluid that was hanging from a metal stand near my bed.

I tried to respond, but could not. She inserted a needle into my arm, connected to a tube that was running a stranger's blood into my body. My limbs trembled and I began to feel nauseous. My abdomen cramped and my head pounded. I gagged and retched just before vomiting blood all over myself and the white sheets upon which I lay.

The nurse jumped back in shock. She shook her head and muttered a curse. "*Merde*." She turned quickly and dashed out of the room, yelling for assistance.

I continued to vomit up the dead blood, my body rejecting it. And once it was gone, I felt even hungrier. I needed to feed on live human blood and I needed to do it soon. It was obvious that a blood transfusion could not save me. I vaguely recalled Victor mentioning that our sustenance must come from a living thing, one of the many lessons he taught me during my time at Bran Castle. Vampires had to feed upon a warm human: we could not inject cold blood directly into our veins. Our bodies did not work the same as mortals. We were biologically different. I never understood how different my body was until that moment.

I forced myself to sit up by sheer force of will. After my head stopped swimming, I pulled my weak legs over the side of the bed and placed my feet on the cold floor, testing my strength. I stood up, using the bed's rail for support, praying that my knees would not give. It took effort, but I managed. I bit back another round of nausea and listened to the commotion just outside my room's door. The nurse frantically attempted to explain my reaction to the transfusion, but was still having difficulty forming coherent words. I heard a familiar man's voice asking her questions and trying to get through her befuddled state.

I did not have much time before they discovered me on my feet. I heard noises in a little room just to my left, a bathroom. Someone was in there urinating. I could nearly smell the blood pumping through their veins. I licked my lips and lunged at the door, which gave beneath my touch.

It was a bathroom. An elderly man sat on a toilet there, spittle dripping from his lips, his eyes hazed over. On the sink next to him was a razor: I grabbed it and pulled out the blade, pouncing on him before he had a chance to react, raking the razor blade across the artery in his neck. Blood welled from beneath his thin skin. I threw myself around him, my legs wrapping around his waist. I tilted my head and placed my mouth over the wound and drank until nothing was left. His old life rushed into me, making me feel young and new. The irony was not lost on me.

The world came back to me in clear focus. I quickly stood up and straightened myself, pulling my blood-covered hospital gown over my legs to appear decent. With one hand, I shoved the old man off the toilet, his body falling to the floor with a quiet thump. I threw the used blade next to him, making the scene appear as if it were suicide. I hurried back to my room just before I heard the nurse and someone else at the door, their footsteps hurried. I stood beside a nearby chair, one hand on the back of it, as if I had been there all along.

The nurse stared at me, her eyes wide when she saw the color returning to my face. I walked confidently to the bed and sat down, noting the doctor standing behind her. He was a handsome man with compelling eyes. There was also something familiar about him, and it came to me. "You," I stated, pointing a slender finger at where he stood. "It was you that saved me."

The nurse, still flabbergasted, said nothing. She might as well have been invisible in that moment.

The doctor's eyes set upon my face. He nodded and answered, his voice gentle and kind. "Yes. The bullet passed through your body and just missed your heart. There was internal bleeding, but... you..." he paused as if attempting to understand the miracle of my health. "You seem to have made a full recovery."

I nodded, demurely, taken in by his tone and his words. "Thanks to you. *Merci beaucoup.* You are my hero."

He held out a hand, ignoring my blood-stained garments, "Dr. David LaRoche, at your service, *mademoiselle,*" he said.

I took his hand and it was as if a bolt of electricity passed between us. It was another one of those little moments when you feel that everything is about to change, for better or for worse.

Little did I know that it would be both.

The hospital insisted on keeping me for several more days "for observation," but ultimately, Dr. LaRoche, who told me to call him David, admitted that I was in perfect health. After I checked out of the facility, he escorted me home that night, back to my apartment in Montmartre. He remarked about the bright pink facade of the building and I explained that the ground floor was a cabaret where I once sang during the occupation. Of course, he wanted to know more, so I regaled him with my heroism during the war, although I left out some of the more unsavory parts of my seduction of the General.

David stayed long enough for a drink of the alcoholic variety and we talked into the wee hours of the morning about nothing specifically, having our own private celebration that the war was finally over. I learned that David served on the front lines, tending to the wounded and sick. I admired him for his bravery, but there was something else, an attraction to him that I could not deny.

In the days that followed, Paris ended its celebration, but a sense of hope and optimism pervaded the air as the city returned to its normal operations. The city was alive again, more than ever, and offered a fresh start for its citizens, and even for me.

My life as a vampire continued, although there were enough Nazis still hiding in the city for me to discover and feed upon. I still hid the bodies, although if they were ever found, the city would not mourn their passing.

The City of Light became the City of *amour*. The world fell in love with Paris all over again, and soon, she was the shining star of Europe, an example of the power of persistence and love. The world shifted and changed, as it always does, but this time for the better. The women who entered the workforce during the war were now valuable members of their countries' economies. They gained more voice and power, demanding equal rights for themselves and others. The end of the war brought on a new age of enlightenment, where men and women could stand as one.

I continued to see David regularly, although I understood that our time was short. I was immortal, or so I believed, and he was not. And what sort of future would that bring us? In the early days of our romance, I convinced myself I would tell him about my condition when the time was right, but of course, it never was. All I really wanted was to remain at his side, to feel his love, to find happiness.

Months passed like that and I was happy. And although I knew wishing that things would stay that way was impossible, I wished for it nonetheless.

CHAPTER SEVENTEEN

It was a glorious autumn day, nearly a year after I first met David. It was the kind of day that makes you appreciate the colors of the season, all the red, gold and brown leaves that drift lazily from the treetops to rest on the Paris sidewalks and streets. David had made plans to take me to the Jardin des Plantes, which housed a zoo, a place I remembered from one of my past lives when I was a mistress to a king. It was intended that the first animals sent to the facility would meet their untimely ends, but the scientists at the facility decided to keep them alive for study and to educate the public on wildlife. Many of the animals that remained there were the descendants of those animals once so beloved by King Louis.

As we walked through the winding trails that led through the area, I told David about its history, leaving out the parts about how I once lived it. I still had not admitted to him anything about my true nature, and it was likely that I never had any intention of doing so. I continued to convince myself that this fantasy was all that I had, all that I wanted, and that I would do nothing that might bring it to an end. Someone loved me and I loved them and wasn't that all that mattered?

The narrow paths led us to the animal enclosures. We stopped in front of the elephants. I loved the big, gray beasts, who were far more intelligent than humans believed. They had a nobility about them, something that I recognized, something that spoke of long lives and wisdom. I related to these animals in a way that no other human could.

As we stood there, the slight stench of dung reached my nostrils, and I wrinkled my nose. The scent did not really offend me, though. I had smelled much worse through those many wars. Even Versailles wasn't above smelling musty, particularly at summer parties with nobles who chose to douse themselves in perfume in lieu of bathing.

David took my hand and pulled me away from the fence so that I stood closer to him. He met my gaze and put his hand in his pocket, reaching for something there. He pulled out a small box and took to one knee.

My heart leapt in my chest as the realization of the moment struck me. I knew where this was going. I knew I should run away now, or at the least, confess that I was not human. I thought that this was a mistake, and yet, I trembled with expectation, my heart telling my mind to forget what I was.

"Reinette, my dearest," he began. "You do know that I love you so. Would you marry me?"

These are the words every little girl wants to hear when she grows up, having already planned her response and the ceremony to follow. Even I, who was never a normal girl, entertained notions of marriage based on love once, long before I learned better, and it was that little girl that answered the question without any thought as to its implications. "Yes," I said, with tears in my eyes.

I should have said "no." I should have told him how ridiculous he was. I should have told him that I was a vampire and that we did not belong together. I should have apologized for allowing him to become so attached to me. And yet, I said nothing but what the love in my heart bid me say.

David caressed my hand as he slipped the ring over my finger.

Even later, as we walked home hand in hand, I questioned my decision. Yet my happiness would not allow me to see anything from an intelligent point of view. I was a fool, but I was a fool in love. And as they say, there are no greater fools than these.

I gave myself time to walk in the clouds after the proposal, but the monster that was my conscience continued to scream loudly inside my head. I could ignore the truth no longer. David and I needed to discuss some very important details, and that included revealing the one thing I did not really want him to know. But I loved him and he had the right to the truth, or at least some semblance of it.

Several weeks later, we sat side by side on a bench in a grassy area of one of the city's many squares. We faced each other as a chill wind from the north whipped loose tendrils of blonde hair around my face. It was a last gasp of fall before winter began to breathe over Paris.

"I need to speak to you about something important," I began as I reached up to move hair from my eyes.

David's expression changed instantly. His face was a mask of concern. "Surely you are not having second thoughts, love?" he asked, his eyebrows furrowed, his gray eyes cloudy.

I shook my head vehemently. "Oh no, nothing like that *cherie*," I assured him. "It is just that you know very little about me and I would have you know more." I forced myself to look into his eyes. "I have a confession to make." In my lap, my hands began to shake.

David, noticing this, took one of my hands and patted it. "I know enough, my dearest," he said. "I know that you are brave and kind and that you love me. Are these things not so?"

Who could argue with that?

I smiled softly and continued. 'Perhaps, although you should know by now that I most certainly love you, with all my heart. But there are things in my past…" I hesitated as I tried to find the right words with which to express myself. This was a speech I had practiced often in my mind, but now that the moment had arrived, my tongue did not want to comply. "Things in my past I am not proud of."

I wasn't saying enough.

David clung to my hand and pulled himself closer to me. "As have I," he announced.

I blinked several times, surprised by this turn of events. This was not part of the moment that I had carefully rehearsed.

David looked down at our hands linked together, as if suddenly ashamed to meet my gaze. "During the war, I saw things, did things," he said. "We all did. We do what we must to survive. To come home. To live. To love." He briefly looked up at me, his eyes the color of the darkening sky. "But all that matters is what happens now, my love. And I do not care about who you were before we met. Now is all that matters. And now, you are Reinette, the love of my life."

I stared at him in astonishment and awe. I did not deserve this kind of love or affection. My mind began to change, as if it were the wind. I decided that I would not tell him what I was, not for fear that he would leave me, but for fear that he would stay, knowing what I was. And that terrified me more than anything.

But there was something he did need to know. It was my turn to stare down at our entwined hands. "But there is something else, and you must hear me out," I said as I squeezed his hand. "I am unable to have children."

It was a little lie, but also the truth. I was unable to have children - with him. I briefly thought of my past life, the one with Victor and Espy. The thought caused me to shudder and let go of David's hand.

But he grabbed my hands and kissed both palms. He saw my distress as a fear of him rejecting me. But my fears were deeper and darker than that. In that moment, I felt my long history bearing down on me as shame filled me with how I had run away. These dormant feelings rose to the surface and lay festering like an open wound in my heart.

David's eyes bore into my soul. "And you think that matters to me?" he asked. But then he paused and took a deep breath. "I, too, have a confession, *mon amour*. I have two sons."

My lover was full of surprises.

"What?" I asked, as I looked up and met his gaze, my eyes widened. The shame from my past floated away from me on butterfly wings.

He nodded and continued. "Yes, my wife left with her family during the war, during the occupation. She took my boys to America and died there. They now live with their grandparents in New Orleans."

How else could I hear this news but with acceptance? After all, I had many secrets of my own. I responded with a smile and squeezed his hands as I leaned forward to place a kiss upon his lips. This was nothing in the grand scheme of things, I told myself. This was a sign that we could marry, that I could have the life I always wanted. The past was just that: the past.

These were only some of the lies I told myself.

"I would like to bring them back to Paris," David added. "With your permission, of course." His face was so serene in that moment.

Perhaps I should have argued against it, but I was deeply lost in the fantasy of the lies. "I would have it no other way," I replied, pushing away all doubts and fears.

It seemed that I would have a second chance as a mother.

David's sons, aged ten and eight, arrived a week before the wedding. David never mentioned why he did not send for them earlier, although I could guess that he did not think I would find myself amicable to playing the part of a mother so quickly.

Honestly, I was terrified. My first and only experience as a parent was a failure, and with the boys, I was not really even a parent, but a stranger attempting to step into that role. For David, though, I was willing to play my part. Surely, he was worth it.

We met the children at the airport. They greeted their father with smiles and laughter rushing into his arms to embrace him. I stood just off to the side while the reunion took place, unsure of how I fit into this instant family.

Gabriel was the first to notice me. "Who are you?" he asked, his smile fading, his eyes narrowing.

When Daniel, the youngest, noticed me, he quickly skirted behind his father's legs, his eyes suddenly swollen with fear. To him, I was a monster ready to devour him.

I shivered, not from the cold, because the day was warm, but because I wondered if children could sense the truth about my nature. I forced a smile and held out a hand to Gabriel. "I am Reinette. And I'm very pleased to meet you."

Gabriel stared at my hand, but he did not take it.

"Boys, I told you all about Reinette," David spoke up as he approached me and took me by the arm. "In my letter."

Daniel continued to hide behind his father, his eyes staring holes through my body.

"Grandmother read it to us," Daniel whispered.

Gabriel nodded, but continued to watch me with suspicion.

"Nevertheless, Reinette and I are to marry," David stated as he placed an arm protectively around my shoulder and began to guide us away from the plane and through the airport.

The boys were silent as we walked down white narrow hallways to the exit. There, we entered a taxi, the children sitting between the two of us.

Gabriel sat closest to me. "You're not our mother," he hissed as he crossed his arms.

"No, I am not," I told him, my fake smile permanently pressed upon my lips. I attempted to convey compassion, trying to hide the fact that I did not much like this little boy.

"You'll never be our mother," he replied.

Daniel clung to his brother, sinking so far into the seat that it was as if he wanted to escape into an oblivion that did not include me.

I stared at David, my eyes pleading, almost filled with tears. This was not going well at all. This was my life, my future, my everything, and it was already falling apart.

"Reinette will be my wife, though, boys, and you should respect her," he announced. "I expect that of you, *d'accord?*"

Gabriel grunted something in the affirmative, but Daniel did not reply.

The taxi wound its way through the chaotic streets of Paris as it made its way to the ninth arrondissement, to the house that we called home. When we arrived, we exited quietly, although I heard Daniel mumble something to Gabriel as David unlocked the front door.

Once the door was open, the boys ran into the foyer and up the stairs that held rooms that I soon learned were once theirs.

David stood with me in the foyer, holding my hand as he watched the boys disappear from view. The sound of doors opening and closing echoed throughout the house. "They'll warm up to you, I promise," he said, his free hand gently touching my cheek. "And they will love you as much as I do."

Even in such a short time, though, I knew better. Because young boys could never love the woman who stole their father away.

For propriety's sake, and for the boys, I insisted on separate living arrangements for David and me for the two months before our wedding. I still rented an apartment near Gare de Lyon, and lived there until the day we spoke our marriage vows. I felt the gesture was important, especially as it gave David more time to focus on his sons. My agreement to marry into the family was more important than my pride.

This was one of my better decisions. As the days went by, it was evident that the boys and I might never have the kind of relationship where they would consider me a suitable mother figure. Gabriel often treated me with outright derision and Daniel continued to keep his distance. They were always present in my life, though, at least when I was with David. These meetings often left me feeling awkward. I found much pleasure in going home at night to my own quiet abode. This made me feel guilty.

My love for David never waned. I loved the smiles that his sons brought to his face. I loved how he loved them and still managed to find room in his heart for me. I loved that he tried to convince them that I was worthy of love, too, although they didn't seem to agree.

I loved the idea of being a part of that family, even if I did not feel as if I yet belonged. The boys were a splinter in my relationship, of course, but time would heal that wound, would it not?

Our wedding day was the happiest of my life. Although I was married once before, I treated this one as if it were the first. I spared no expense in making it as perfect as possible. I hired one of the best Parisian fashion designers to create my dress, which was a beautiful gown of ivory and lace that cascaded past my feet and behind me in a long trail. I ordered white roses for my bouquet, dotted with green ivory, colors I felt represented the life I now wished to live.

Although David never understood my need for extravagance,

he indulged me. Money was no object because of the many smart investments I had made throughout the years. He did not even balk when I insisted that we marry just outside the Cathedral de Notre Dame, the only church I had ever loved, not because it was a house of God, but because of its beautiful architecture. David did not question the long list of people I invited, including his family, as well as those friends I made during the war. Our marriage would be the social event of the year.

I fell into planning, loving it as much, if not more, than any party I ever once planned at Versailles.

Everything fell into place during the ceremony. Gabriel acted as ringbearer, while Daniel scattered petals along the carpet before my entrance. Both boys were in good spirits, and I told myself that this was a sign of their changing attitude towards me. Perhaps I would not become a mother figure to them, but they now had to admit that I would become their father's wife.

I listened to breaths caught in guests' throats as I walked down the aisle, gliding down a red carpet on a path that led to my beloved. Once together, we took each others' hands and said our vows, promising that we would love each other forever in the eyes of God (who I never had any use for) and the world.

We sealed that promise with a kiss and followed that with a grand party at the Petit Palais.

I moved back into the house with David, while the boys spent the evening with friends. Our lovemaking that evening was slow and deliberate, the kind that happens between two people who planned on spending the rest of their lives together.

David eventually fell asleep, leaving only the quiet house and myself awake.

Even on the most happiest of days, my thoughts would not give me rest. I pulled myself naked out of a bed that smelled of musk and sex and stood by the window, letting the lights of the city bathe my skin. I stared at the city, at *my* city, so changed from when I first grew up here and yet somehow completely the same.

Thoughts about the future began to haunt me, dancing around my head like demons.

Someday, David would grow old and die. And I would not. I knew instinctively that this is something I should have talked to him about, and I promised myself that I would, a promise I had made every day since we first met.

I convinced myself that it was different now that we were man and wife. I would certainly find myself capable of delivering the news, and he would accept it. It was only a disease, what I was, a thing that he, a doctor, would certainly understand.

But it still did not change the fact that one day, I would have a life without David. And such thoughts tormented me like insects that only come out at night. In my mind's eye, I saw his face growing old and wrinkling, his hair turning gray, while my youth and beauty remained constant. The boys would become teenagers and then adults, but I would stay unchanged throughout those years.

Humans are like leaves. They are beautiful things that don't last very long, only to become more colorful just before death. Then they die and fall to Earth, replaced by other leaves.

Except that there was no replacement for David.

I looked down at stared at the simple gold band around my finger. "'Til death do us part," took on an entirely different meaning in the dark of night.

I could leave. I could sneak out of this room and the door. I could run away again. I could leave another note, urging David and the boys to move on without me.

But I would do no such thing. I was selfish. I loved David too much. I wanted happiness. I wanted a family and a chance to live a life I was never permitted to have before.

I could not help what I was. So did my being a vampire really even matter?

I stared at my reflection in the dark window dotted by the lights of Paris. I made a decision. I would say nothing and stay.

David stirred in his sleep with a soft mumble. I turned to look at his handsome face, my mind made up. Whatever the future held, whatever I chose to share with him about my true nature, I was his.

I had decades before I needed to worry about these things anyway, decades we could spend together before it became obvious that I was not mortal. And in that moment, those decades seemed so far away that I convinced myself that my current worrying was ridiculous.

I tucked my fears deep within my heart and locked them away and in that moment, I was happy.

CHAPTER EIGHTEEN

That happiness remained for some time. In the few years that followed, even the boys grew to accept me in their father's life. Of course, this wasn't the same as obtaining their love, but for me, it was enough. Our family was happy. I had hope for the foreseeable future.

But hope has a way of running out. Even after several years of wedded bliss, my secret began to grow and fester inside my heart like an open wound. I found it harder to separate the vampire part of myself from the part that pretended at mortality with David, because the truth is I was ever only one person to begin with.

I found ways to take care of myself, though. Every Thursday evening, I met with a women's group at the Bibliotheque Nationale to discuss the important issue of the day and how they related to the feminist cause. On one Thursday of each month, though, I would leave the house as if going to that meeting, but I would never arrive there. Instead, I used that evening away from home to hunt for prey.

It was deceitful to use those meetings in that way, and even more deceitful when it involved lying to David. But I did it anyway, because I soon realized that I would probably never tell him the truth.

Paris was full of evil men and women that stalked its streets. These were individuals who never seemed to have people looking for them, so when they disappeared, they were rarely mourned. It was not difficult to seek them out and drink my fill, hiding the bodies where I could: in the sewers, in the river and in the many forests surrounding the city. Those few bodies that were found, though, were so well-decomposed that they were unrecognizable.

I left a trail of victims behind throughout the city, in hidden places that only I remembered from the past. That was one of the benefits of having lived so long: I knew Paris better than any other living soul in the city. Eventually, I stole a key to a crematorium at Père Lachaise: I took to burning the bodies of my victims, leaving no trace that they had ever existed.

On one particular spring evening, I took my time returning home after feeding, preferring instead to walk through the Tuileries to enjoy the scent of the flowers blooming there in the warm spring air that promised that summer was on its way. There was still a coppery taste on my tongue, the blood I'd taken running warm through my arteries.

At the house, though, David met me at the door. "Madame Vintnier stopped by to check on you," he said, his eyebrows furrowing anxiously. "Apparently, she thought you were not feeling well and told me that you missed tonight's meeting."

My legs began to tremble as my mind working feverishly to find a response. Madame Vintnier was a known busybody, a woman who spent a lot of time sticking her nose in other people's business. She had no intention of checking on my health. I was sure that she was spying on me to see what I was up to when I did not make the women's club meetings.

Calmly, I smiled, terror hidden deep behind my eyes. I moved slowly as I took off my hat and coat and hung both carefully on a rack we kept by the door. "Oh, well," I answered, hoping my voice did not betray my panic. "I decided that I would rather have a walk in the Tuileries this evening. It's such a lovely spring evening and I could not resist. As I had no real excuse to skip the meeting, I told them that I was sick." It was a lie that was not a lie.

Racked with guilt at my falsehood, I stared at David as innocently as I could, batting my eyelashes and tilting my head.

David was a gentle and trusting soul. He nodded and took my hand. "Of course. It is lovely. But next time, perhaps you should invite me?" He turned my hand over and kissed my palm.

"Of course, but it was a spur of the moment decision," I lied.
David smiled and the world spun back into clear view. But
there was something nagging deep within me, a realization that
made the lying all that much worse. When I lied to David, I knew
that he would respond with kindness. That was his nature.

And in knowing that, I was the worst kind of monster of all.

Although guilt tore at my heart, I continued to lie to David
about my monthly hunting schedule. Our lives were so settled,
so good, that perhaps it was far too late to admit to him that I
was a vampire. I ignored all warnings in my gut that told me
otherwise. On some days, I thought that perhaps I would tell
him, but I didn't, always putting it off until the next day, the
next week, the next year.

When I stared at myself in the mirror, I saw a face that never
aged, never changed.

David did not seem to notice my never-changing beauty,
though.

I noticed his. Little lines began to grow around the edges
of his eyes when he smiled. Little dots of white appeared in his
hair around his temples. Time marched on for him, a mortal.

The boys began to grow and change, too, with Gabriel well
on his way to becoming a man. Daniel grew several inches in
one summer, and it was obvious that both boys would become
tall like their father. Gabriel was already becoming handsome,
with his dimples, curly locks and wide brown eyes. But Daniel
looked more like his father, with reddish-brown hair that always
looked mussed and serene blue-gray eyes. Even Daniel's facial
expressions reminded me of David: the way he narrowed his
eyes when deep in thought, the way his whole face lit up when
he smiled.

The boys' temperaments were also different: Gabriel still
harbored some resentment towards me, although he was
mostly amenable when I was around. But I saw it in the way he
grimaced when I asked him to do something. Daniel, though,
began to open up to me, and even took to holding my hand in
public.

A year passed after I nearly got caught in my lie, but there were no other incidents, no more busybodies at my door informing my husband that I was not at the meeting I had planned to attend. I drank my fill when I was hungry and carefully took care of the bodies after.

I pretended that my life was normal and good.

Perhaps it was, at least for a time. But as always happens, the extraordinary found me once again.

It was September, 1948. Memories of the war began to fade and the city of Paris grew, becoming more alive than ever. There was an excitability in the air, the kind that comes when people regain hope and optimism.

David and I, along with the boys, were at a large fair in the Bois de Vincennes. It was a carnival with games of chance, sideshow freaks and rides that would make people dizzy should they stay on them too long. There were booths selling crepes, both savory and sweet, as well as roasted nut vendors and artists showcasing their latest pieces. Street musicians with accordions, guitars and flutes played happy music, while a monkey on a chain wearing a cap danced for tips.

Gabriel, now too old to spend his precious time with adults, ran off early to join friends, hoping to win his weight in prizes by tossing rings and throwing balls at jars. Daniel stayed behind, holding our hands as his eyes grew wider with each spectacle we saw. He marveled over a magician doing tricks with cards. He looked on in wide-eyed wonder as a woman with a beard stood on a stage.

David and I indulged him as we discussed the possibility of taking a trip to the Riviera later in the year. The three of us walked slowly, sauntering down the carnival's main thoroughfare.

It took me several minutes after seeing the bearded woman before I realized that Daniel was no longer holding my hand. I saw the top of his head in front of us, though, right before he dashed in front of a couple and disappeared from sight.

"Daniel!" I called out as I watched his small figure slip away. A strange panic gripped me, unlike anything I was familiar with. Dread creeped across my body, like a dark cloud does before rain.

David, noting my anxiety, took my hand. "He's fine. We'll

see him later," he assured me, his finger rubbing the back of my thumb.

But that unexplained feeling gripped me tightly in its invisible fist. I began to push my way through the crowd, one hand on David's arm, pulling him behind me. My eyes wandered over the scene, searching for the small boy who I suddenly feared for.

I led us to a small circular tent. From within, the sounds of circus music played, somehow sounding ominous. I pulled us into the heart of a crowd standing at the edge of tiered steps that held seats, scanning the crowd with my eyes.

In the middle of the tent, elephants danced in circles and did tricks. The people on the stands cheered and applauded.

A cold sweat broke out across the backs of my arms. I stood there as the trainers, and elephants, took their bows.

"That's all, good people of Paris," a man dressed as the ringleader announced. "Merci and bonsoir!"

As the show came to a close, the crowds inside the tent stood and began to exit. Someone brushed by me, their shoulder colliding with mine. I turned around quickly, but only caught a glimpse of a young woman with long blond hair.

There was something familiar about her, I thought, right before she got lost in a sea of humanity.

Something tugged at my skirt. I looked down to see Daniel standing there. Relief washed over me.

Everything was okay. Why was I so certain that he was in danger? Looking upon him, he was fine. What could explain my irrational fear?

"Reine," he said, his pet name for me. "Wasn't it wonderful?"

I nodded as I kneeled, bringing myself to his eye level. "You shouldn't run off like that," I told him, my breath heavy from my previous excitement.

"I'm sorry, Reine, but you found me, didn't you?" he asked.

"I did," I answered. "But you must promise not to do that again, without telling me where you are going."

"But you were here anyway," he stated plainly. "I saw you sitting up there." He pointed to a spot in the middle of the stands, which were now empty. "I saw you laughing at the clowns. You liked them so much!" He laughed.

I didn't laugh. I leaned forward and tilted my head. "I did not see any clowns. I was standing near here," I replied, confused.

Fear. Dread. The familiar blond woman.

Daniel shrugged and took my hand. "Can we get ice cream now? I would like some ice cream, please?"

David approached from behind me, putting an arm around my waist. "Ice cream for three coming right up!" he announced as he took my arm and led us out of the tent.

After filling our bellies with ice cream and fond memories, we forgot the incident. My mind, in its self-preservation, buried any real, or perhaps even imagined, appearance of a strange, yet familiar woman. By the time we arrived home that evening, all was well and comfortable again.

With the weeks that passed, the colors of summer began to fade as the hues of autumn stole in on the wings of birds migrating south for the winter. A breeze blew in from the north, adding a fresh chill to the air, the kind that makes one think fondly of warm sweaters, wool coats and warm scarves. We began to spend evenings curled up in blankets, drinking tea or hot chocolate, as fall began to embrace us in its cool embrace.

This new cold, though, brought change to the house, as well as sickness, striking the youngest among us with a cruel illness that David believed was the flu. Certainly, young Daniel's symptoms were similar enough to warrant such a diagnosis, but after several weeks, there was still no recovery.

Both David and I grew concerned, although my concern was much darker. There was something recognizable in Daniel's suffering that I related all too well with. The boy was so pale that he was nearly white and although he complained of a constant hunger, he rarely ate, turning down most meals brought to him. I tried to dismiss my increasing worry as paranoia, but as the boy began to waste away and other doctors failed to properly diagnose him, my sinking feeling continued.

I began to ask the question: what if Daniel was like me? What if he was a vampire? I attempted to dismiss these thoughts as quickly as they arose, but as each day passed and Daniel came closer to embracing death, I could not deny the truth.

Of course, there was one way to find out for sure. I could bring Daniel a body full of blood and have him drink from it.

But what if I was wrong? What if his disease was not the same as mine?

But if I was wrong, what would it hurt to know for sure?

Ultimately, this was the question I chose to answer. On one clear and chilly morning, with David at work and Gabriel at school, I enticed a man into our home, a man I knew who had Nazi sympathies, and someone no one would really miss. I seduced him into thinking that he would join me in the bedroom, when I, in fact, presented him to Daniel right before I pulled out my ever faithful little knife and slit his wrist.

The man cried out as I pulled him towards the boy, still somehow convinced this was part of a little game we would play before lovemaking. I placed his wrist against Daniel's lips. "Drink," I whispered.

Daniel latched on to the man's arm and bore down with a strength I had not known he possessed. Blood poured into his mouth as I sat, watching, envious, remembering my first taste of that old Romanian woman so very long ago.

I stepped back as the man struggled and began to flail about, but Daniel's grip on his arm persisted. Eventually, the man went limp and fainted, but still the boy drank. And he did not stop until the man was dead.

It was only then that the boy loosened his grip and let the man slide to the floor where he fell in an unimportant heap. Daniel's cheeks flushed pink, the first color that had come to his face since his illness had taken him.

"Oh, my dear sweet child," I uttered as I kicked the body under the bed, making a mental note to remove it later. I stroked Daniel's forehead, which felt cool beneath my fingertips. The fever was gone.

Daniel smiled at me, his eyes clear and healthy. "Je t'aime, Reine," he said.

Perhaps I didn't realize it before, but once he said the words, I knew that I had longed to hear them. "Oh, my darling, je t'aime, aussie." I stroked his hair with my hands as tears flowed from my eyes, both in joy at his recovery, but also in mourning for what his life would now become. His childhood was gone, replaced by something much darker. But I had his affection, and in that moment, all was still well.

Downstairs, the front door opened and closed with a solid "click." I heard the quiet laughter of a woman.

Daniel started, hearing it, too.

"It's just the maid," I announced, although I later remembered that it wasn't her day for cleaning. But my thoughts ran in circles, as they do. I thought about the body under the bed and the chance that someone could discover it. I stood up and arranged my clothes, pulling one edge of a sheet up over Daniel to cover the small blood-stained marks on the bed.

There were footsteps on the stairs, light and sure.

"She's coming," he said, his eyes wide, frightened.

I nodded, uncertain of why he suddenly seemed gripped with terror. "It's just Beatrice," I said, as comforting as I could.

He was fond of Beatrice and often kept her well after her she had finished her work to have her tell him stories she remembered from her youth.

But as the footsteps grew closer, goosebumps ran up and down my arms. I rubbed my elbows with my hands, dismissing it as a chill brought on by the fall weather.

I knew better, though. "Who? Who's coming?" I asked Daniel.

The footsteps stopped just outside the boy's room. There was more laughter as the scent of vanilla mixed with musk wafted into the room, the same scent I once wore so very long ago in Austria.

I knew that laugh. It was exactly as I remembered it: like a bell ringing off-key. My little knife was still in my hand. I gripped it tightly in my fist, raising it up.

The door to Daniel's bedroom swung open. Espy stood there in the doorway, smiling, looking almost exactly like me, right down to her choice in clothing. She was grown now and most certainly my equal. There was a mature intensity in her eyes and in the way she stood with one hand on her hip, studying us and the scene.

"Hello, Mother."

Time slowed, then stopped as I stared at the woman in the doorway, the woman who was also my daughter. It was like looking in a mirror, although Espy's hair was a little lighter in color, more like her father's. But her blue eyes were darker and burned with a fire that I did not possess.

But it was still as if I was facing myself. Perhaps I was.

As the past came rushing at me, I felt my knees go weak, but by some miracle, I continued to stand. My body felt paralyzed, though, and my mouth was speechless, almost too afraid to even take a breath.

Daniel, too, was also silent, as if he understood the importance of this meeting.

As Espy moved into the room, I also could not help but think that she looked sane. Could it be? She walked with the gracefulness of a dancer, her long legs pulling her body to the sweet rhythm of a song that only she could hear. She stopped in front of me.

When she smiled, it was if I were in Austria again, staring at my sweet darling girl before the bloodshed, before the murders.

Here was the girl that I had abandoned.

As shame washed over me, I cried, bowing my head and covering my face with my hands. This was a truth I had denied for so long, but now it faced me and I realized that I was wrong. I was always wrong. Centuries worth of guilt filled my heart, which ached unlike ever before.

Espy reached up and pulled my hands away from my face, using two of her fingers to force my chin up to look at her.

I did, but it was so hard. An ocean of tears poured from my eyes.

"Mother, it's okay," she said. "I'm here now. Everything is okay."

Although her words seemed comforting, I did not understand.

"I am so sorry," I finally blurted out, spittle flying from my lips as waves of sorrow and anguish washed over me. My shoulders shook as I sobbed and my hair fell into my face as I clenched my hands at my sides, unsure of what to do with them.

"I forgive you," Espy whispered softly as she bent closer and kissed me on the cheek.

Words can have such power, especially when they are words that you longed to hear without ever even knowing it.

"I understand," she added as she took a few steps back and took in the measure of the room, waving one hand in the air. "I was a horrible little creature. I was a monster. You did what you thought you had to do."

I stared hard at her, my mouth agape. I believed every word she uttered. How could I not? She was the fruit of my loins. She was my only child.

Daniel finally found his voice to speak up, "Reine? What's happening?"

It was Espy, though, that answered him. "It's okay, little one," she said as she strolled over to where Daniel lay on the bed. She leaned over him and wiped at the tiny droplets of blood that stained his mouth with her thumb. "I am Reinette's sister, and we were once estranged, but now we're not." She turned her attention to me. "Isn't that, right, dear sister?"

I dumbly nodded.

"Oh, that's nice," Daniel whispered as he closed his eyes, the warmth of blood he had just consumed enveloping him in sleep.

"That's right, Daniel," I said. "You get some rest."

I took Espy's hand and led her out of the room, closing the door behind us. I walked us down the corridor and into a few rooms over. This room was a small library and office, the place where we kept our collection of books and important documents, including our certificate of marriage that hung on the wall.

"Really, Mother, it's fine. I'm fine," Espy said to me, squeezing my hand before dropping it. She scanned the room with her gaze, her eyes lingering briefly on the document that hung on the wall.

I suddenly remembered the day of the carnival, which seemed so long ago. "That was you," I said. "At the fair."

Espy turned to me and nodded. "Yes. Of course, I knew about the boy." She gestured in the general direction of Daniel's room. "I knew what he was. So I followed him."

"You were... following us?" I asked, inexplicably a little frightened. I took a few steps away from her.

"I was following him," she explained. "I had no idea he was attached to you in any way." Her hands moved in the air as she spoke. "Imagine my surprise when I saw you there, too. It was fate, dear mother. It was fate telling us that it's time to make amends."

I opened my mouth and then promptly closed it. Perhaps she was right. It made sense. Victor was able to find vampires among humans, so wouldn't it make sense that our intuitive daughter would also have that ability?

It was an ability that I, obviously, did not possess. Otherwise, I would have known about Daniel.

I sat down, once more wracked with guilt. My hands clenched in my lap. I could not find words to respond to her, to make the amends that she required. I did not deserve forgiving and I certainly did not deserve love.

Espy knelt on the floor beside me, "It's what I do. I have spent the past few decades finding others like us. To help them. To make sure they know what they are. To help them adjust to this... life. But when I saw that Daniel was with you, my heart burst with joy."

How could I deny her this reunion? How could I deny her anything? I was the absent mother, the woman who left her behind. And yet, here she was, forgiving me and offering not just her compassion, but her love.

All evidence of the Espy that I remembered, the crazed insane little girl that I had run away from, was gone. Instead, here was a beautiful, intelligent and wonderful woman who had somehow managed to become that way without me.

As if sensing my thoughts, Espy laid her hand on top of mine. "Like I said, Mother. I forgive you. I only want to be your darling Espy again. Can we do that? Can I be a part of your life once more?"

How could I refuse her now? "Yes, of course," I told her, wet tears clinging to my face. I looked up at her.

Droplets shimmered within her eyes. "We'll keep our secret,

of course, if that is your wish. I am merely your sister come to visit. Only we will know the truth."

I nodded. She had thought of everything. I did not even question how she knew about my not telling David about what I was. Perhaps I did not really want to know. I merely wanted to exist in this moment when all of my wishes had finally come true.

"I do not wish to uproot your life, after all," Espy said. "You seem happy. Are you happy, Mother?"

"I am now," I answered, my gaze taking in all of her, seeing the woman that she had become, a woman very much like myself. I took her hand and squeezed it. "I am so happy now."

"Good," she said, her smile filling the room with its light.

In my guilt, grief and newfound joy, I stood up and threw my arms around her in a warm embrace. "I love you, my darling, Espy. Forever and always." I meant every word.

"And I, you," she answered, returning the hug.

Although I was the prodigal mother in this tale, it finally felt as if my daughter was the one who had come home.

CHAPTER NINETEEN

Espy was a godsend in the weeks that followed. She helped me explain our nature to Daniel, having an even better understanding of vampire nature than I did. Perhaps that was because of her time with her father, but it was more likely due to the fact that she spent years studying vampires and finding others like us after she left Austria.

She did not, however, mention her time with her father, except in passing. She assured me that he was doing well, but that his lab and experiments still took up much of his time. When I asked how long it was since she last saw him, she shrugged, but did not offer an answer. Instead, she told me about the things she learned away from him and her country of birth. I learned much from her about our kind and realized that although our condition was rare, we were not the only members of our species.

That's what she called vampires, a species. She agreed with Victor in believing that we were something other than human, something mutated from humanity.

That is a matter on which we often debated. I always considered vampirism a disease, a curse bestowed upon us by mother nature. But after my daughter shared her discoveries on her journeys, I began to understand our kind differently.

However, I still felt very much like a human.

I often wondered why I never sought out others like me. Perhaps I always thought that they did not exist. But perhaps I had sought out others, without even realizing it. How could coincidence be the reason that my stepson was also a vampire, too?

Of course, I had not known Daniel when I met David, but it seems that something, perhaps fate, guided me to this family. Had I subconsciously known that my marriage to David would lead me to more of my kind?

The hardest part of Daniel's awakening, though, was keeping up the lie with David. Daniel showed a new maturity in understanding that he could not explain to his father what he was and agreed with both Espy and I that it was best keeping this a secret. We organized secret plans, ways of explaining away our monthly feedings, although three victims per month meant that we had to take more care in how we fed.

Despite that, though, all was well. David took to Espy as my sister and treated her as a part of the family. He even occasionally remarked that I seemed lighter, more full of joy, in her presence.

This was true. I was happier than ever. My family expanded, past and present, in a way I had never imagined. Isn't this what I had always wanted?

David never even questioned Daniel's miraculous recovery, although he certainly had questions. I could see them in his eyes. He was a doctor and could not comprehend how quickly his son came back from the grips of what was certainly death. He was so grateful about Daniel's survival, though, that he never asked those questions.

Perhaps it was not a perfect life, not with the blood and lies, but it was a life. We lived and we thrived.

Paris came alive in a new way that winter, in a way I did not know that it could. By Christmas, there was snow on the ground, blanketing the city in a white purity as the streets lit up with the colorful lights and garb of the holidays.

Another year passed and then was gone.

January stole in during the wintry nights, making our breaths icy and our faces flushed from the cold.

But lie began to pile upon lie as Espy and I snuck Daniel away every month, making excuses each time that sounded so hollow to my ears. Guilt ate away at my heart, especially as I lay beside David each night, staring at a ceiling that was part of my home.

David, though, never questioned a thing. Perhaps he did not want to.

Gabriel, though, did. The older boy began to make inquiries, remarking that Espy and I spent a lot of time attending to Daniel. He even went to his father with his concerns.

David even asked me once why we seemed to flood Daniel with special treatment over the eldest. I explained that it was because Gabriel was at an age where he did not wish to spend time with his stepmother, a woman he never really wanted to care about in the first place. That much was true as I had previously asked Gabriel to join me at the library and the museum, being turned down each time.

But Gabriel suspected something, I knew. I could see it in the way that he carefully watched Espy and me. I could also see it in the way he treated his younger brother. Gabriel was an intelligent boy, and he certainly saw that something was going on. He grew ever more suspicious with each passing day.

Espy and I reached out to the oldest boy on more than one occasion, but each time, he refused us.

But he still stayed close, too much so at times. We caught him eavesdropping on conversations, fortunately innocent ones, on more than one occasion. He slinked around the house and hid around corners to watch Daniel as he did his homework or as he played.

David even informed me that he caught Gabriel trying to sneak out of the house after us during one of our outings with Daniel.

"He feels left out," David attempted to explain a few evenings later. He was just arriving home from work late that night, sitting on the bed and taking off his shoes.

I sat at the vanity, staring at my unchanging face in the mirror. "But he won't go anywhere with me," I stated. "Or with Espy."

David stood and paced over to me in socked feet. He placed his hands on my shoulders as we stared at each others' reflections. "Maybe if you offer to do something with him that he likes?"

I shrugged and sighed. "I've offered to take him to the theatre and to the movies. He likes those things, but not with me."

David squeezed my shoulders. "He likes reading."

I looked down, staring at the hairbrush and perfume bottles on small shelves. "And yet he won't join me at the library," I answered, my voice rising slightly in frustration. "He does not like me. He never has. He never will."

David leaned over and kissed the top of my head. "That's not true," he said, but his eyes told a different story. David knew that Gabriel would never accept me and that it was something we both accepted as reality. But my husband would never admit it, at least not to me.

I stared at David through the mirror.

He looked away.

Something broke inside me, like a dam filled with holes that finally gave. A flood of emotions burst into my heart and surged their way to my tongue. "There is something I need to tell you," I whispered, almost hoping that he wouldn't hear me.

But he did. He drew closer, the lines across his forehead furrowed.

I noticed the wrinkles around his mouth and his eyes first, the kind of lines that my face would never have.

"What is it, love?" he asked, rubbing my arms. "You can tell me everything."

So I did.

David learned about my life as a vampire, as a courtesan and as a mistress to a King. I told him about Victor and explained that Espy was not, in fact, my sister, but my daughter. I even explained why I left Austria, assuring him that Espy was different now, calmer, more mature, safe. I admitted that I murdered others to survive, but explained my personal creed to only feed from those who I felt really deserved it.

David stayed quiet throughout my explanation, the expression on his face dark and unreadable.

Once I had finally stopped talking, he spoke. "You're a vampire," he said, his voice barely above a whisper, as if somehow saying that sentence summed up the entirety of my life.

It was my turn to remain silent. There was nothing more to say.

"And you tell me that my son is a vampire, too?" he asked, his head moving back and forth as if trying to sort his thoughts out and make sense of my story.

I continued to say nothing as I sat at the mirror, too afraid to face him, only daring to occasionally glance at his reflection.

David's expression finally changed. His lips dropped into a frown as his eyes narrowed. He stared down at his hands and clenched them in front of him. When he looked up, I did not recognize him as the man I loved. Anger changed him, unlike anything I had ever seen as he stared at me not with love, but with hatred.

"I don't know what you're playing at," he spat at me, his arms dropping to his sides, his hands still formed as fists. "Or what you've dragged my son into. But this is not funny. This is not amusing. This is… this is just a crazy little game and…." He brought his fists up and stared at them. "It's wrong. You're wrong. Do you understand?" His voice rose as he spoke, each word louder than the last. He took a few steps closer to me, his feet landing heavily against the floor in his rage. "I won't stand for it. How dare you? I took you in. I brought you into my family. I trusted you. I let you into my heart! Is this fun for you? Is it? Why would you do this? To me? To us?" He violently began to gesture around the room, his temper flaring.

I swallowed hard and stood up, finally turning to face him. I did not know this man screaming at me, this man filled with so many angry words, denial and rage. But again, this was what I feared all along, what I thought could happen if I told him the truth. I had convinced myself in a moment of weakness that he would accept me as I was, but here was my worst fear come to life. No matter how much David loved me, no matter how much any human ever loved me, they would always betray me when they found out what I really was.

Telling him was a grave mistake. But it was too late now. And because of my error, I would pay the ultimate price.

My perfect and happy life was over.

Maybe it was for the best, I tried to tell myself. This

conversation was fate: it needed to happen. I was still an immortal, one who would not age. Did I truly want to watch the love of my life grow old and die? Sooner or later, he would know the truth regardless. Now was as good a time as any.

But I had more to think of. There was Daniel to consider. If David denied that his son was a vampire, the boy would surely grow ill again. And although I was not as invested in David's sons as I was in their father, an immortal lifetime of prolonged starvation and suffering was not something that I would wish upon anyone.

But I did not have a chance to even ask about Daniel or even to plead with David to see reason.

"Get out," he said, almost whispering it.

I could not move. I opened my mouth to speak, but words would not come. I wanted to say so much, to warn him about Daniel, to apologize, to beg for him to forgive me, for all the things that runs through the mind but not through the lips in such situations.

"Get out!" he yelled, more forcefully.

His words cut through me, like daggers in my heart. They prompted me to action. I closed my eyes and reached for that place that I knew that kept me safe, where my heart sat behind a wall where it could not suffer. I forced tears away, my eyelids acting as a dam against the flood. I held my head high and walked slowly to the bedroom door and opened it.

Espy stood there, biting her lip, one hand held out to me. She had heard the entire exchange.

I reminded myself that I was not alone and that I still had dignity as I took her hand and walked through the doorway. I took a single glance back to see David with his back turned, his shoulders shaking as he sobbed.

I did not bother to gather my things. Instead, I walked with Espy away from David, from that room and from that house without another word.

One month passed and then another. Espy and I attempted to create a new life in an apartment in the 12th arrondissement near Gare de Lyon. It was smaller than the house David and I had shared, but Espy and I each had our own bedroom, which made it just large enough. I chose it based on the fact that it had a dark blue painted door, and for some reason, that door seemed to represent to me what my future held: sadness and despair.

Espy tried to talk me into leaving Paris altogether, but I would not hear of it. I still felt a need to stay relatively close to David, in hopes that perhaps he might change his mind. I could not tear myself away from him so readily, even after he shunned me from his life.

I also worried about Daniel, who was now an immortal alone in a mortal world. With David denying his nature, I feared that he would not survive.

I also could not leave Paris, the city that I loved so much. I feared that leaving her would destroy me. This was my home, and it held many memories for me, both good and bad.

Espy called me stubborn, but soon learned that I would not budge. And for some reason, she, too, chose to stay.

I did not understand why, though. I was hardly an attentive mother or even a friend to her in the time that passed after our move. I was lonely and miserable and often took to fits of despair where I insisted that I could not bear to go on for another day.

Espy, though, was a good daughter. She did everything she could to keep my spirits up. She scheduled us appointments with stylists and fashion designers. She insisted I leave the apartment and go with her to museums and galleries. She dragged me to the libraries and book stores so that I could learn more about the new up and coming writers of the time. She introduced me to the words of Georges Duhamel, Ernest Hemingway and Agatha Christie. And although I found temporary enjoyment in these things, my sour mood would always rear its ugly head when we returned home.

I had no more happiness, no more hope, except for in those little things that I found fleeting. Perhaps this was my way of punishing myself for my dilemma, which I surely caused by all my secrets and lies. I told myself that had I explained my condition to David sooner, I would still find myself embraced in his arms as a part of his life and that we would carry on until death claimed him.

I also could not help but think, though, that our separation was the hand of fate, although the bizarre twist of Daniel becoming a vampire was not something I, nor anyone, could have possibly foreseen.

David was the love of my life and now, he was gone.

Espy eventually grew tired of my melancholic demeanor and spent more time away from the apartment and me. She began to disappear for days at a time, indulging in parties and cabarets and whatever it is that young Parisian girls do to prevent boredom. She always returned to hunt with me, though, but our time together grew quiet, as if we no longer had words to say to each other. In retrospect, perhaps she blamed herself for events, too. Or perhaps my mood was just contagious, infecting everyone around me with its sadness.

Life has a way, though, of coming around full circle. Espy and I had a rare evening together, discussing philosophy and our take on *For Whom The Bell Tolls* when a knock on the door interrupted our lively discussion. A feeling of dread came over me in the form of a prickly feeling across my flesh.

Espy casually got up, on bare feet, and sauntered to the door in that way that always made me think of her as a dancer. She swung it wide open, letting a chill draft float in from the long hallway from beyond.

I was on the sofa in the living room, clinging to an unopened book in my lap.

Familiar footsteps, a tread I knew well, echoed across the hardwood floors and stopped just short of where I sat.

"Reinette?" David's voice filled the room with a timbre that I had nearly forgotten about.

I looked up and stared at him, suddenly wondering if I had fallen asleep and was deep in a dream.

David looked worse for the wear, though. His usually tidy clothes were wrinkled, his tie askew. He had circles under his eyes and looked far older than I remembered. When he knelt beside my chair, he was slow about it, as if every bone and joint in his body ached. His eyes, though, were as intense as ever, burning through me with their fire.

Although I wanted to tell myself that this was the reunion

I had hoped for, I knew that it was not. He was not here for me. "Daniel?" I asked.

David nodded and reached up to touch his tie, clenching it in his hand. "He is... ill again. Wasting away. I am..." he closed his eyes briefly, unable to say what he needed to. "Like you said. He is not well. And I am willing to believe you if you can help him. Can you help him? Can you make him better?"

The pleading in his voice tore at my heart. I could never bear to see my beloved in such pain.

I straightened myself and placed the book on a side table. I pulled his hand away from his tie and squeezed it.

He did not return the affection.

"He needs to feed," I said, letting my eyes wander over his haggard face.

Espy stood behind David, biting her lip, her eyes narrowing as she watched the scene.

David nodded and pulled his hand away. "I do not claim to understand. I am sorry. I am sorry that I did not believe you. I am sorry that I let it come to this. But he his unresponsive and dying. Please help him, Reinette. Please help my son. If you still love him... if you still love me... please."

Love does not fade even after relationships end. So I agreed quickly and stood up, motioning for Espy to grab my coat from a nearby closet.

The girl jumped into action and fetched my outerwear. As she helped me into it, she spoke, "I know of a man, a rapist." Her eyes darted back and forth between David and I.

David cringed as he listened to her words. His face screwed up in disgust. As he stared at us, he only saw two murderers, regardless of whether those getting murdered deserved it or not. And he understood that his son was like that, too.

"This man, is he close?" I asked Espy, trying to maintain my composure under David's judgmental stare.

Espy took my arm, "I'll show you."

I approached David where he stood and placed a hand on his shoulder. He shrugged my touch off and stepped away.

Here was yet another reminder that he was here not for me, but for his son.

"Go home," I told him. "We'll take care of it. And when we arrive, hide yourself and Gabriel. We will slip in and out. It will be like we were never there."

A small sigh of relief escaped his lips. At least he now knew I would not have him witness a murder. He turned around quickly and exited the apartment, nearly running out the door.

"Quickly," I told my daughter as we set out for the evening in search of prey for David's son.

Very few words passed between Espy and me as she led me to the home of the intended victim, a man she called Monsieur Fournier. She briefly explained how he often took advantage of young women, luring them to his home, where he would proceed to rape them. He got away with these deeds because his victims were often already prostitutes and looked down upon them as women "who were asking for it."

Such was the way of the world, as it often still is.

Monsieur Fournier answered his door almost immediately after we knocked on it. There was a sly grin on his face, an expression that reflected a man who got away with whatever he wanted. We explained that we were new to the city, and after a day spent wandering its many chaotic streets, we were lost. We told him that we needed a guide to escort us back to our house in the ninth arrondissement, where we lived alone. We assured him that we would hold nothing but gratefulness if he could help us and that we would offer him a cup of tea at the end of the journey.

He smiled and stared at us luridly, surreptitiously wondering about his sudden good luck.

Monsieur Fournier led us to the nearest Metro station, pretending himself a gentleman. We regaled him with praise and teased his sense of virility and manhood. He insisted on walking us out of the station at St. Germain des Prés and to the house we indicated that was ours, which was, in fact, the house I once shared with David and his sons. By then, the man was nearly licking his lips in anticipation of the deeds he would serve upon us.

But he had no idea what deeds we had planned for him.

We arrived at the house and invited him in. The door was unlocked, allowing the three of us to enter easily. Somewhere in that house, I imagined David sitting quietly, sobbing into his hands as he came to grips with the truth of what I had told him. I tried not to think too much about this, though, as we led Monsieur Fournier up the stairs to Daniel's room.

Espy opened the door and shoved the man inside.

"What is this?" he demanded to know, his good humor changing as he fidgeted with the waistband of his pants.

Espy closed the door behind us and smiled, bringing the tip of her finger to her mouth. "You'll see." She winked.

The man grabbed at her bosom lustily.

Espy played along and allowed him to touch her.

I cringed, thinking that his touch must feel grimy and oily.

She drew him closer to the bed where Daniel lay.

Daniel was still, very little life left in him. His time was short.

Monsieur Fournier never even noticed the boy, though, so caught up he was with Espy, grabbing at her greedily, one hand roughly pressed against her breast and the other shoved under her dress.

I stared at Espy, willing her to hurry. Disgust rose like bile in my throat as the man continued to grope her.

Espy pulled a knife from a hidden pocket in her dress. It was similar to my own little knife, its intended purpose the same.

Monsieur Fournier never saw the attack. Espy was so quick and savage in her motion that blood swelled from the slit in his throat before he even realized his injury.

He let go of my daughter and brought both hands to his neck, blood spurting through his fingertips.

Espy grabbed his head and shoved him down onto the bed, the font of blood directly over Daniel's mouth.

Daniel drank, his throat swallowing over and over, the blood filling him and making him whole. He did not stop until Monsieur Fournier lay dead and the man's body slipped to the floor.

I heard footsteps downstairs, David's. I prayed that he would not allow curiosity to bring him to this room to survey the scene. But he certainly heard everything that transpired here.

Espy kicked at the body until it was out of her way, a forgotten husk that once treated women as playthings.

Although I did not mourn the life lost, I found her treatment of the body harsh and unnecessarily cruel.

She placed a hand on Daniel's forehead, smiling at him. "There, there, little one. You're all better now."

She spoke truth. Daniel's cheeks flushed with new color. He beamed at Espy and reached out a hand to me.

I quickly came to his bedside and took that offered hand, holding it and feeling the warmth return to its skin. But I also could not help but see the bloody mess surrounding us. "We must clean this up," I stated.

Espy wrinkled her nose and stood upright, shaking her head. Her face held no expression as she looked at me with a gaze that chilled me. "I've done my part." Then she turned around and without another word, exited the room. She said a quick "au revoir" to David downstairs right before the front door slammed behind her.

Daniel sat up as he squeezed my hand, his face covered in blood that wasn't his, his sheets soaked in the crimson substance.

It did not matter, though, for he was well. Yes, life would never return to normal. But I did what I had to. I wrapped the body in Daniel's bloodied bedclothes. I emptied the trunk that sat at the foot of the boy's bed and dumped the body into it. I dragged the trunk down the stairs, grateful for its wheels, waving David away, not wishing him to witness any part of this. I grabbed the keys to David's car on my way out of the house and drove to the Montparnasse Cemetery, where I burned everything to ash in the crematorium.

Ashes to ashes, dust to dust.

When I returned from this jaunt, David met me in the foyer of what was once our home, falling to his knees at my feet. *"Mon cherie,* forgive me. I did not understand. I did not understand this secret that you've carried all your long life."

I looked upon him, exhaustion seeping into every pore of my skin. "Do you understand now?" I asked, daring to hope for this to have a positive outcome.

David stood up and took both my hands, not minding the

specks of gray ash littered across my skin. "Yes, my love. I do. Please come home."

I responded by nodding. But after months of despair, it was still hard to find joy in the moment. "You cannot tell anyone, David. You cannot tell them what I am. Or what Daniel is. You cannot even tell Gabriel. He, among everyone, must not know."

David's head moved up and down, desperation written in the lines of his face. "I will share this secret just with you and Daniel. I will help you both carry it. It is ours and ours alone."

An old adage says that you can never go home again, but that night, I did.

CHAPTER TWENTY

Coming home, though, was not as perfect as I thought. Although I believed that Espy added something' special to our happy family, even with our secrets laid bare, she did not agree. Instead, she insisted that she would remain on her own to live in the apartment that she and I most recently shared.

"But why?" I asked her after returning to that apartment to gather up some of my things, mostly books and a few knick knacks. I picked up a copy of *Animal Farm* and placed it carefully in a box.

Espy did not answer immediately, but seemed perplexed by the question. "I do not..." she began, her voice trailing off as she organized her thoughts. "I am a grown woman, an adult. And I think that perhaps it is best if I were to live on my own." She cleared her throat and shook her head. "You have David and his sons. You have a life. Perhaps it is time for me to begin a life of my own." As she spoke, she brought one hand up to look at it.

Her hand trembled, but I hardly paid much notice to it.

"But you are a part of my life now," I attempted to explain. I placed the box down carefully on the sofa to approach her, reaching out to take one of her hands.

Espy drew back, placing her hands behind her back. Her face changed, became expressionless, completely unreadable. "Perhaps. I need my own life. My own love. My own time." Her voice suddenly sounded adrift, as her thoughts were anywhere but in the present.

I wrinkled my nose as I tried to ascertain her meaning. Her words seemed a little jumbled, but I still shook them off. I did realize that she was immovable in this decision, though. I recognized a stubbornness in her that reminded me of my own.

"I cannot say that I am not disappointed," I responded as I walked back to the sofa and stared into the box and then back at her. "Will you stay here in Paris?"

Espy shrugged and raised the corner of her lip. "Maybe? There is still so much world to see. Maybe I will go see it. Or maybe I will go check up on Father. Or maybe I will go the Americas. I do not know. I just need... I need..." she paused as she struggled to find words, but words seemed to fail her. Her left eye began to twitch, as if her tired brain had worked too hard. She moved to sit down in an armchair, her hands clenched in her lap. She swayed back and forth, as if unable to sit still. She looked at me, but also through me, as if she saw something in the distance, beyond the walls of the apartment.

Something began to itch at the back of my skull, but I chose to ignore the sensation. "Well, I would miss you terribly," I told her as I returned my attention back to my box of books and porcelain figures. "But you do know that you are welcome at our house at any time, don't you?" I looked up briefly for her reaction.

The far-off look in Espy's eyes faded away and she focused her attention on me once more. A smile spread across her face, and it was like when sunlight pierces through a dark cloud. She was a charming creature, much like her mother. "Of course, Mother," she answered. "I will visit. I promise." She beamed at me, her body as still as a doll.

But the cloud moved in again over her face and her smile wavered. There was something dark just underneath the surface of her expression. However, I did not take time to assess this brief blemish of personality. Instead, I responded with a *"bien,"* and placed the box underneath my arm as I walked to the door, ready to make my way out.

Espy reached out and lightly touched my arm. "Until later, *maman. À bientôt.*"

I did not think further upon my conversation with Espy until several days later. It was then that I realized that something about it bothered me, but I could not say exactly what. I also did not have time to dwell upon it, though, because my life at home was also not without its issues.

The situation with David was good, better than I expected. We became affectionate with each other again. Perhaps it was because the truth was lay bare between us now. There were no more secrets or lies.

But that did not mean that David did not have questions. I could see them in his eyes when he thought I was not looking. But these were questions he seemed fearful to ask. Surely, he understood that I would answer them now, with a truth I had not before, but until he was ready to approach the subject, I said nothing.

I understood that these things would take time. I was sure that him discovering that his wife and son were vampires was no easy thing to wrap his mind around. He obviously struggled with the concept of what we had to do to survive. He already knew about my previous life, as Madame de Pompadour, but that did not mean that he had a comprehension of everything.

When he was ready to ask those lingering questions, though, I would answer.

The real problem in the house was Gabriel. At 14, the boy took to rebellious acts and spent much of his time arguing with his father. He barely spoke to me, and mostly, I was grateful for that. When I was in Gabriel's presence, his usual response was to pretend that I did not exist. There was a cold derision around him, even more with my return, as if he were truly happier during his father's separation from me.

Gabriel, who once adored his younger brother, became increasingly distant from Daniel. He did everything he could not to spend any amount of time with him, preferring the company of his few friends. I thought maybe it was because of Daniel's fondness for me, and I for him, and that somehow, Gabriel felt as if his brother betrayed him in that. I tried to understand that maybe Gabriel just felt alone in the world, but reaching out to him was all but impossible.

Life changed, as it does, and I did my best to work with what I had. I did what I needed to do. I played the role of wife and surrogate mother with as much patience as I could muster, reminding myself that this something almost lost to me and remembering gratefulness that it was not.

Yes, Gabriel was a large problem, one that David and I often discussed. On one spring afternoon, several months after my return, the subject came up again. David and I sat together on our bed, staring out of the open window of our bedroom. Green leaves dotted the limbs of trees just outside of it and a warm breeze sifted in with the promise of summer.

David brought the topic up first. "I've been thinking about Gabriel," he said as his fingertips massaged his forehead. "About boarding school. Maybe it isn't such a bad idea."

I frowned. This was not a new discussion. "He would hate you for it," I remarked, knowing that was the truth. Boarding school for the teen was originally my idea, but when I thought about it, I realized that it might make our difficult situation even worse.

"He keeps asking me questions," David said as he gazed at me, his expression dark and clouded. "About you and Daniel. He knows that you are both different somehow. He does not say it, but I feel he knows." His hands clutched the edge of the bed.

My face softened, but I said nothing.

"These lies, Reinette," David whispered as he shook his head. "They are tearing our family apart." His lips curled down slightly, sadness etched across his features.

"Gabriel was always suspicious of me, though," I reminded him. "Even before." It was true. The boy never liked me.

David let out a deep breath. "I don't know what to do."

The sound of a commotion followed by a loud crash came from downstairs, interrupting our conversation.

We jumped to our feet, springing into action. We exited the bedroom and rushed downstairs. In the living room, a vase lay broken on the floor, the table that it once sat upon turned over. Daniel lay beneath his older brother, pinned by Gabriel's weight. Gabriel's teeth bared as he hissed at his brother, his fist raised as if he might punch the younger boy in the nose.

"Stop!" Daniel screamed, his fists hitting his brother in the chest.

Gabriel acted as if he didn't feel a thing.

David approached the boys, while I remained standing at

the bottom of the stairs. "Just what is the meaning of this?" he demanded.

Daniel bit his lip as if he wanted to say something. Tears pooled in his eyes. But he remained quiet, as if somehow, he still wanted to protect his brother, who clearly was at fault.

David grabbed Gabriel's hand and pulled him away, lifting the boy to his feet. He glared at him. "How dare you? How dare you attack your brother like that?"

Gabriel spat at his father, his voice screaming, echoing around the room. "I don't belong here! I'm not like you! You're all... monsters. I hate you!" He turned his head and looked at his brother. "You're not right. You're different. And it's all because of her!" He looked at me, a finger pointed accusingly in my direction.

I backed up until I felt the stairway's banister press against my back.

Daniel sat up, his eyes narrowing. When he spoke, his voice was low and menacing. "I will kill you. I will slit your throat and drink your blood."

A shudder crossed my body as I remained frozen in place. I did not even look at David, but I could imagine the horror he felt as his youngest son's words hit home.

"See? He's a monster!" Gabriel exclaimed, pulling away from his father's grasp and fleeing, running up the stairs, his feet loudly hitting each step all the way up.

"Daniel!" David hissed at his youngest.

I watched the scene unfold, a hand brought up to my mouth.

Daniel's face contorted into a mask of tragedy. His held tears began to pour over his rosy cheeks. The pitch of his voice raised as he pleaded. "I'm sorry, Father. I didn't mean it. I didn't mean it." He looked at me. "I didn't mean it, Reine. I just... I just said it. But I didn't mean it."

A wave of conflicting emotions washed over me as I found myself rushing to his side. I knelt on the floor beside him and scooped him into my arms, clutching him to my chest.

David remained where he was, staring at us. And for just a few seconds, I saw him look at us the way that Gabriel had. In that moment, he saw us monsters.

Perhaps we were.

CHAPTER TWENTY-ONE

Despite the incident, we fell back into the routine of daily life. David went to work. I attended the openings of art galleries and bookshops. The boys went to school. On the surface, everything seemed normal, although when we were all in the house, the tension was like a weight pressing down upon me.

I did my best to ignore it, though, by going through the motions, and hoping that things would become fine in the end. Isn't that what being human is all about? I had the important things: a home, a family and David's love. Everything else did not matter.

At times, I even quietly entertained fantasies of bringing Gabriel into our big secret, thinking that maybe we could win him over by including him. Of course, my imagination always played the scenario out to an unhappy end, because I could not deny that the boy seemed to hate me more with each passing day. He blamed me for so much, perhaps even his mother's death. Perhaps he believed that I was the devil in every part of his life.

Gabriel also spent less time with his brother. Family dinners were awkward and way too quiet, although David and I both did our best to keep matters light and make harmony when we were together.

But there was no denying the cloud that hung over our house: a storm brewed just beyond the horizon, lying in wait to claim us. I felt it as if it were a physical object that I saw coming at us and threatening to wipe everything away. But each time that feeling came over me, I ignored it, willed it away, willed myself to just be happy.

I was selfish and I wanted my perfect family so badly that I chose to not pay attention to the storm headed our way.

I begged Espy to visit, wanting to include her in my delusions, but she always declined. She had excuses of being busy with new studies or hobbies, but I never believed her. Each time I saw her, she seemed much lonelier than before, in need of a family she no longer seemed to want. She never shunned me in any way, but I often felt when standing in her presence, she wished that I would just go away.

I, however, continued to invite her into my life. I felt it necessary to paint the picture of the life I hoped to achieve. Eventually, she finally acquiesced and agreed to go to a performance of "Much Ado About Nothing" with our little familial unit. It was one of her favorite Shakespearean comedies, that being the very reason I chose it, hoping that she simply could not refuse with her usual excuses.

Espy showed up at our door early on the evening of the performance in a beautiful pink lace dress that made her seem like an ethereal being, something from another plane of existence. Her mind seemed elsewhere, though, when I greeted her with a kiss on each cheek. Her eyes darted back and forth as I took her hand and brought her into the living room.

David was in the kitchen, pouring himself a pre-theatre drink.

I excused myself to rush upstairs so that I could finish dressing myself. I chose a modest long dark green dress, a gift from David, bought just for this affair.

The house was aflutter with activity, with life. A sense of something filled the air, although maybe I mistook it for anticipation and delight.

"Boys!" I called out as I worked my way down the second floor hallway, knocking on bedroom doors to urge them along. "We'll be late! Please hurry!" I heard the ticking of the grandfather clock on the landing, marking our tardiness, an antique from the life of David's grandparents.

On the first floor, a glass fell to the floor and shattered. The ticking of the clock slowed and came to a stop.

My breath caught in my throat. It felt as if something had

sucked all the air out of the house. Anticipation turned to dread, which launched me into running down the stairs, taking two steps at a time. One of my slippers fell off, but I paid it no heed, leaving it behind as surely as Cinderella did when fleeing her ball. Fear filled my veins as I entered the living room, stopping for only a moment to survey the room. I saw nothing.

The coppery scent of blood filled my nostrils as I slowly walked to the kitchen. I heard a suckling sound that I knew all too well.

At first, I averted my gaze and stared at the light on the ceiling there. My eyes watered and filled with spots. It was only then that I looked down at the floor, where David lay motionless, surrounded in blood, his throat slit open, Espy's lips attached to his neck. I stared at his chest, willing it to move, but it did not.

David was dead.

"Get away from him!" I screamed as I hurried to my daughter and began to beat my fists against her back.

Still, Espy continued to drink, her pink dress now soaked in red.

"Dad!" Gabriel's voice cut through the din. He stood just in the entranceway of the room, his eyes widening as he saw what was left of his father laying on the floor.

Gabriel's voice grabbed Espy's attention enough to convince her to finish her meal. She looked up and stared at the boy, grinning through her bloody teeth. But she spoke to me, her voice gurgling from the blood still left in her throat. "I had to do it, Mother. He was a bad man. He took you from me. He was a bad man."

I barely heard the sound of small footsteps on the stairs, coming down. But Daniel's voice carried through the house. "Where is everyone?"

I felt a combination of fury, rage, heartache and pain. "Get. Out. Get. Out. Get out!" I screamed at the woman in front of me, the woman who I once called my daughter.

Espy blinked and stood up. She shrugged, her eyes wild, her expression completely mad.

"You're a monster!" Gabriel screamed from where he stood, his fists clenched at his sides beating at his thighs.

Daniel appeared behind his brother. I turned to face him. He looked at his father laying dead on the floor. Then he looked at Espy, her face and dress smeared with blood.

I ran to the boys, facing them, my body blocking the horrific view as much as it could. But it was too late.

Gabriel stared up at me with pure hatred in his eyes. "I will kill you for this. I will kill you and I will kill her," he hissed through gritted teeth. He turned around, shoved his brother out of the way and ran out the front door. Outside, I could hear him screaming for help.

My thoughts numbed as instinct took over. I grabbed Daniel's hand and followed Gabriel out of the house. But I took us in the opposite direction.

That marked the end of my perfect life, my perfect family.

CHAPTER TWENTY-TWO

Sirens blared behind us as we ran, but we managed to get far enough away from the house to prevent suspicion. I dragged Daniel behind me through the maze of the city's streets, not stopping until we were well past rue d'Alesia and I was certain that no one followed.

I ducked into a small and dark courtyard, pulling Daniel with me, both of us out of breath and sweating. The humidity of the summer night weighed heavily upon us, but it was the events of the evening that haunted our thoughts. As I tried to calm my breathing, I attempted to pull my mind away from what we had witnessed, forcing myself to think rationally. Letting emotion rule us would not see our safe escape from Paris. I needed my wits, so I pushed everything to the side as I began to formulate a plan.

Daniel remained silent, probably still suffering from shock. I was grateful for his silence because I was not capable of answering questions then and it would only slow us down to have a conversation.

My mind seemed to circle around itself, but, eventually, I decided upon our next course of action. Our priority was to leave Paris, but that required resources and money.

I turned that thought into action and began walking casually down the street, maintaining a false air of calm, just a mother and her son out for a stroll beneath the stars. I stopped at the first phone booth we came across and carefully placed a call to my accountant, a man I trusted with all my financial affairs. In a matter of minutes, he agreed to direct funds to make them quickly available to me. In just 20 minutes, he had a messenger deliver what cash I needed to tide us over. He never asked why, which was, essentially, what I paid him for.

Once we had cash in hand, Daniel and I made our way to the train station at Montparnasse. The boy remained perfectly calm as I arranged for a train to take us to Calais. From there, we quietly took a ferry to Dover, where a train to London waited for us. Daniel slept through most of the journey, exhausted and spent, but I could not. Instead, I stared into empty space, finally allowing myself to embrace the horror that we had witnessed.

I asked myself all the questions: had Espy really killed David? Or was it just some nightmare that I would soon wake up from? Why did I not see this coming? Was this somehow my fault? Were we, in fact, what Gabriel called us, monsters?

The journey was not incredibly long, but it felt like days when we finally checked into a hotel near Victoria station in London. Once we found ourselves settled in our room, the dam inside Daniel finally broke. He looked at me with tears flowing over his rosy cheeks, asking the same questions I had already asked myself. "Did Espy kill Daddy? Is he really dead?"

I fell to my knees in front of him and wrapped him in my arms, resting my head against his shoulder. "Yes, dear, I'm afraid the answer is yes." I realized that this was more of a reply for myself than for him. "And I am so sorry, so very sorry." What more could I say?

"It is not your fault," Daniel responded, pushing me back so that I could see his tear-stained face. "I love you, Reine."

I noted that he used David's pet name for me almost immediately. And in that single moment, I could see David, and not his son, staring back at me. I blinked through my own tears until the illusion faded.

"Please do not ever leave me," he pleaded, his small fingers digging into the tops of my shoulders as if he would cling to me for life.

"Never, Daniel," I answered, my arms encircling his waist. "I will always be here. Always."

How easily I made that promise to him when I could not make that promise to my own daughter. But I meant it, every word.

I would never leave Daniel. He was all that I had left of David.

That was the last time we discussed the events surrounding David's death. Instead, we let time pass and allowed memories to fade, along with seasons and years. Daniel and I stayed in London for a few months, but spent the rest of our time traveling around the area, spending time in York, Wales and Scotland. Eventually, we made our way to Ireland and took up residence in Dublin.

Fourteen years passed quickly. I watched the timid boy that was Daniel grow up and become an awkward teenager, but then a tall and confident young man. By the time we settled on the Emerald Isle, he was in his late 20s.

And he looked so much like David that it nearly hurt to look at him.

Perhaps hurt is too strong a word. There was an ache in my heart, but there was also a longing, in a way that made me feel ashamed. It wasn't just that Daniel looked like David, but that he was also a handsome self-assured young man and vampire, someone who had not let the tragedy of his youth define who he was.

It was often Daniel who chose our victims. He had a good head for finding the lowest of society and sniffing them out, investigating their lives and routines as if he were a spy sent to watch over them. When he hunted, he was like a hawk, his eyes never leaving his prey, although he remained stealthy, never seen until he was ready to strike. I often accompanied him and found myself entranced by the way that he moved through Dublin's streets on feline-like feet, his movements quiet and graceful.

Watching him caused feelings to rise in me that should not have. I also feared that he felt the same. But what could one expect when two grown adults only spent time with each other?

I denied those feelings, but they persisted. I convinced myself that to act upon these emotions was improper. Not only that, but I still held a sense of duty towards his father, a man dead because of me. It was bizarre, perhaps wrong, this odd relationship between Daniel and me. But although we were stepmother and stepson, we were hardly part of a traditional family unit. Now that our physical ages were similar, I remembered that I was a woman and that he was a man. Such urges were natural, weren't they?

Daniel, though, felt more strongly about the sexual tension between us, although I did not know it until later.

One evening, after hunting and drinking from two murderers, suspects wanted in a bank robbery, he made his intentions known. We were high on the blood life, holding hands as we walked together down the dirty streets of the city, nearly skipping along as we made our way back to the small apartment that we shared, a flat that sat on the second floor above a building that housed a pub.

The sounds of people drinking and making merry, laughter and singing followed us up the stairway that led to our home. Daniel unlocked the door and opened it wide, motioning me to enter first.

I did.

He followed, closing the door behind him. He leaned against its wooden surface and reached up to wipe a few traces of blood droplets from his lips.

We still held hands.

Daniel pulled me closer so that our faces were nearly touching. I could feel his breath against my forehead.

"I love you, Reine," he said, his voice husky, nearly growling.

For a moment, I thought David returned from the dead, but the tone of Daniel's voice reminded me that this was not David, but his son. Something forbidden hung in the air, tempting me. But I tried to hide my arousal as I answered him, keeping my voice flat, controlled. "And I love you."

Between two ticks of a clock, something drew us together. Our lips met, enclosing our mouths, our tongues darting back and forth, touching and exploring, going to that place that makes lovers swoon. Passion and blood flowed through my body and sent a surge of pleasure into every nerve. Thoughts floated away in bliss. All that mattered was this.

Daniel's hands moved across my neck and over the thin

fabric of my dress, pulling it apart at the front. His hand slipped beneath to touch one of my breasts.

My breath caught in response to his touch as my fingernails clawed at the back of his neck, pulling him closer, wanting, needing him as close as physically possible.

But then a flash of light went off inside my mind, sobering me, pulling me out of the moment and back into reality. This was not David. This was Daniel. And this simply could not happen. I quickly pulled away, pulling the front of my dress back over my exposed bosom. "No, we cannot do this," I whispered. My ragged breath betrayed me, though. I wanted this, more than anything. All I wanted was to wrap myself around Daniel and never let go.

But I could not have it. Although I daresay I really understood why.

"Reine, I know you feel the way that I do," he replied, reaching up to run both of his hands through his hair in frustration.

His father used to do that.

"You are my stepson," I said, although I did not think that was the reason why I could not go through with it.

"We are vampires," David reminded me. "We are beyond simple human morality."

These were words I said so long ago myself, and perhaps, they were true. I held my hands behind me for fear of reaching out to him, as they desperately wanted to do. "I am sorry. I cannot be with you like this. I love you, Daniel, I do, but I will not lay with you." And then I lied. "I do not love you like that."

Of course, he saw through the lie: how could he not? Every part of my body seemed to betray me by trembling in lust.

"But you do, Reine, you love me," he insisted. He remained leaning against the door. "I see the way you look at me. Even now. I know you feel the same. It has been so long, my love. How long will you remain faithful to my father's memory? Because he's dead. He is only that: just a memory." His voice rose, but only slightly. Like David, he rarely yelled.

I turned around, unable to face him, unable to face the truth. He was right, and yet, I somehow needed to cling to the notion that he was wrong. Perhaps it was as he said: I had not lain with a man since David. I was faithful to someone who was long gone.

Daniel grunted and opened the door. I shifted my position so that I saw him turn and walk away out of the corner of my eye. The door slammed behind him.

I stared at the closed door for several minutes, as if that would somehow will him to return.

He would return, of that I had no doubt, and when he did, we could go on as before. He would not bring the subject up again and I would pretend it never happened.

Which I knew, quite suddenly, was something I could not do.

In a fit of emotion, I flung myself at the door and swung it wide open. I looked down the stairway and saw a figure of a man walking up in the dim light of the street lamps. Thinking it was Daniel, I ran down the stairs, but stopped when the light illuminated the man's face.

It wasn't Daniel.

It was Victor.

The shock of seeing my old companion nearly sent me over the edge of the railing. I had a moment to decide between fight or flight, although every impulse within my body screamed for me to run. This evening had already held so much emotional turmoil that I did not desire anymore.

I steadied myself as best I could and took a deep breath, forcing myself to look up. I made my face into a mask devoid of emotion. I smiled politely and even offered him my hand. I made it seem as if his visit were a welcome surprise and not an event that made me wish I could completely sink into the depths of the earth never to return.

Victor looked ragged. There were dark circles beneath his eyes, as if he had not slept in days, even months. Although his apparel was clean and untorn, it was wrinkled, suggesting that he had not changed clothes in several days due to the stress of travel. His pallor was pale, even more than usual. His eyes were bloodshot and red. There were lines around his mouth, cutting deep into his face. He stared at me for a moment before he took my hand and kissed the back of it, as if he were an old courtier come to call.

My long history came rushing back at me, once again nearly knocking me off my feet. But I maintained my footing as I turned around and gestured for him to follow me up the steps to the apartment.

Within my heart, though, I still thought of Daniel, although I did not allow that concern to show.

"Come in. Welcome. It is good to see you again, old friend," I announced as evenly as I could. I led him into the main entryway into the flat.

Victor looked around, his lip curling, taking in his surroundings, perhaps seeing Daniel's coat haphazardly dangling from a coat rack, a sign that I did not live alone. "As it is you," he replied.

"How did you ever find me?" I asked, trying to keep my voice light. I led us into the living room, motioning for him to follow. I indicated a large rose-colored sofa for him to sit on.

Victor shook his head. He did not sit down. This was not a social visit. "Espy."

My smile faded upon hearing my daughter's name. I did not make a sound, but Victor noted the immediate change in my expression.

"I know what she did, Reinette," he said, folding his hands carefully in front of him. "But you do not understand. She is ill. Her mind... it is not as it should be."

I stared at one of the many fleur de lys patterns that graced the room's wallpaper. I listened, although I hardly wanted to. This was a topic I longed to forget. Espy was the source of so much of my pain, both past and present. I did not speak.

"She's in trouble," Victor said. "That's why I'm here." He stared at me with sincerity, his eyes glassy and sad. "There's an organization. They call themselves the Knights of Christ. And they hunt us. They hunt vampires. They have our daughter."

Any other mother might react differently, but to me, my daughter was as good as dead. So I shrugged, because I would not allow this conversation to mean anything to me. "And how do you know that?" How could I care that she was in danger? Every day, I remembered the sight of her leaning over David's body, drinking his life away.

Victor continued to speak. "I was in London investigating the group when she went missing. Their leader is a man by the name of Gabriel LaRoche."

My hold on the world slipped and began to tumble out of control. I gripped the edge of the sofa and guided my way to sit on it, as if it could save me from the raging seas that now rolled around me.

Of course, Gabriel had grown up to hunt Espy. She had given him every reason to.

Victor explained, "I need to rescue her. And they're here. In Dublin. I need your help. You know this man, you can help."

I shook my head back and forth, loosening blond tendrils of hair from my carefully styled chignon. My answer was fast and decisive. "Why would I help her? She destroyed everything I cared about."

Victor frowned as he sauntered across the room to sit next to me. "He will come for you, too. And for Daniel."

I did not ask how Victor knew so much about me or Daniel, or my life since I left Austria. I assumed Espy had told him, though. Perhaps she followed us after we left Paris, just like before. And that was a thought that made me angry: how dare she come anywhere near me after what she had done?

I moved away from Victor, unwilling to even allow our legs to casually touch as we sat together. "I'm sorry. I cannot help. I have not seen Gabriel in years and we were hardly ever close," I replied. "If you want to save her, you must do it yourself."

The front door opened and closed. When I looked up towards the arch that led from the hallway and into the living room, I saw Daniel. He walked in with his head down. "Reine, I'm sorry. I know I...." His voice cut off as he looked up and saw Victor.

He only knew Victor from my vague descriptions of him, but Daniel recognized him just the same.

I stood up and walked to Daniel, choosing to stand by his side. "Victor was just leaving," I announced.

Victor's frown consumed his weary face, but he did not say another word.

Instead, he walked past us and placed a card in my hand. Then he left the apartment, and hopefully, our lives.

"What did he want?" Daniel asked, eying me curiously.

I looked at the card, which had the name of a hotel on it. I dropped it to the floor and took Daniel's hand. My smile was genuine. "Nothing important," I said. "Nothing important at all."

CHAPTER TWENTY-THREE

Much remained unspoken between Daniel and me, but I did tell him about Victor's visit and conversation. Daniel frowned and shook his head as I explained the meaning behind Victor's appearance in our home.

"You made the right decision," Daniel told me, his voice quiet, barely above a whisper. It was if he understood that my turning down Victor was also my way of choosing him over my own daughter.

That was my reasoning, too: there was no choice, just the right thing to do. My daughter was a monster that I could not control, and I possessed a love for Daniel that superseded any maternal bond I shared with Espy. I cared for Daniel more than I cared for Espy. It was selfish of me to feel that way, but I could not deny the truth I held deep within my heart. I had no regrets in not helping Victor save my daughter.

After that night, life in our home became familiar again. We returned to our usual affairs, although a cloud of sexual tension hung over our roof. At times, I thought it would break me, and I knew that, eventually, I may very well give in to desires I thought forbidden. It was another selfish thing, to allow myself to even entertain such notions, but then again, I was a selfish woman. David was dead and I was a woman with needs that went beyond feeding once a month. I had an appetite and desires, as well as a wonderful man willing to fulfill those wishes and share that with me.

Being immortal was a lonely life, but with Daniel, I need not feel that. I could have something with him I never could have experienced with his father.

Daniel never said a word, though, or hinted that our relationship had changed. But I would often catch him gazing at me with longing. He waited patiently for my stubborn nature to crack, as certain about it breaking as I was.

Only a month passed before that time came. It was late afternoon and suddenly, the dam broke: I had a change of mind, one that encouraged me to embrace my whims and desires. Daniel was not present that morning, having gone out to see a famous author speak at a local book shop. I remained home, already beginning to plan for a romantic evening upon his return. I had not said anything when he left, but I believe the lingering kiss I placed on his cheek gave me away. He walked out of the door with a sly smile: his expression was that of a man about to get what he wanted.

I took the few hours he was gone to bathe in perfumed waters. I dressed myself in thin white lace. I waited on my bed for the man that I loved to come home.

But Daniel never returned. Hour after hour ticked by and Daniel never walked through the apartment to find me laying there, ready for his embrace. Eventually, I fell asleep on a half-made bed, only waking when the morning sun began to stream through the windows.

I panicked upon awakening, quickly jumping out of the bed and wandering through the apartment calling out Daniel's name.

There was no reply. He was still not home.

It was then that I remembered Victor's visit. I also remembered Gabriel, the boy who had promised not just to kill Espy, but also me. But he would not dare attack his brother, would he? But if his organization hunted vampires, then that put Daniel in as much danger as me.

I tried to convince myself that I was jumping to conclusions. Daniel was just out doing something, perhaps still talking about literature with friends. Perhaps he completely lost track of time.

It was unlike him, though, and I knew better. I remembered his smile upon leaving, the one that told me he could not wait to return to me. There was a warning bell sounding off loudly inside my head. I could not ignore it.

I quickly dressed, not even bothering to pull back my hair. I tore out of the bedroom and through the apartment like a thing possessed.

"Where is it? Where is it?" I cried out to vacant rooms as I began emptying out drawers and cabinets. I looked under cushions and behind pillows, but to no avail.

Fortunately, I found what I was looking for casually lying on the kitchen counter: the card Victor gave me upon our last meeting. It probably sat there for a month, long forgotten. I picked it up and read it quickly. "Hotel Brennan," I said aloud, turning the card over to glance at the back. There, something I had not noticed before, was a number. 502. A hotel room number.

I quickly grabbed my purse, shoving the card inside of it. I exited the apartment in a hurry, taking the steps down to the sidewalk two at a time.

If Daniel was actually in trouble, I knew I needed one thing: I needed to see Victor.

Knocking on the door of Victor's hotel room was one of the hardest things I had ever done. I was there, ready to admit defeat, ashamed of my previous dismissal of him and his claims about Gabriel and the threat posed to our kind by the Knights of Christ.

However, I did not fool myself into thinking that I was also there for Espy. This was all about rescuing Daniel, but if that meant also saving my daughter, then so be it.

I did not doubt that Victor would question my reasoning or my purpose, but he would insist that this plan work in both our favors. We both had something to lose here: people that we greatly cared about.

Yes, I believed that Victor cared about Espy. I saw it in his eyes when he first came to me. I was not sure when he developed such a love for our daughter, but perhaps the two grew closer after my departure from the castle so long ago in Austria. Knowing that made me feel only slightly better in my guilt that I did not care about our daughter so much.

Victor did not even feign surprise when he answered the

door and saw me standing there. He gestured for me to come inside.

I stepped through the doorway and took a moment to look around the room. An unmade bed lay behind him, sheets and blankets tangled from whatever nightmares Victor suffered from.

"I think they have Daniel," I said, wringing my hands anxiously. "Gabriel, that is. Gabriel has Daniel."

As soon as I finally said it aloud, I believed it. I'm not sure how I knew the truth, but it was there in my heart. I knew that Gabriel was finally in a position to fulfill the promises he made the night of his father's death.

Victor nodded and closed the door behind me. As he walked through the room, I noticed how ragged he look: his posture slumped and his hair was unruly. His clothes were even more dull and wrinkled than before.

"I know where Daniel and Espy are," he announced, motioning for me to follow him over to a small desk that sat near a window. The surface was covered in hand-scribbled notes, maps and books. Victor pointed to a map of Dublin, showing me a specific location. "There. It's an old warehouse. Most believe it abandoned. I do not."

I stared at the map, unsure. "How do you know this?"

Victor looked at me, his eyes empty, almost like black holes. "I am not without my ways," he answered.

I believed him. "Let's go save them," I remarked and quickly turned around to make my way back to the door, expecting him to follow.

He did not.

I turned on my heel quickly and impatiently, my gaze narrowed.

"Reinette," Victor said as he lifted his arms and stared at his hands. "We can't just blindly go in there."

He sounded frustrated with me.

I huffed in defiance.

"I have already scouted the building. There are highly advanced security protocols in place there. They have an entire group of people working for them and we just have us. We cannot just walk in and demand that they give up their prisoners."

I shrugged as if none of that mattered. All that I wanted was to get Daniel back. I didn't care how much danger I put myself in to accomplish that.

"This group is an offshoot of the Templars," he said.

I shook my head, "The Templars are long dead," I casually waved my hand in the air, brushing off the thought.

"That's what they want you to think," Victor told me as he reached over to the desk and held up a book with a single red cross on it. "But they continued their mission and Gabriel found them. And they love their secrets, puzzles and locks. We cannot expect to access this building without knowing what we are getting into."

It all seemed so ridiculous, and yet, I still believed him. But I also needed to find Daniel at once. I crossed my arms and frowned. "Then what do you suggest we do?"

Victor shuffled through his papers and maps and pulled out a long sheet covered in grid marks. He held it up so that I could see what it was. A blueprint.

"I managed to get this from one of the building's caretakers," he said.

I moved closer and squinted at the paper, which marked several floors underneath the warehouse. Markings showed a series of doors, locks and alarms.

"We study this carefully," Victor explained, tapping the paper with an index finger for emphasis. "And then we figure out how to get in and out of there with Espy and Daniel."

Perhaps he was right, but I had another idea. "I know how we get in there."

Victor raised an eyebrow, but said nothing.

"We use me as bait," I announced, as if it were the most sensible thing in the world. "Gabriel wants me, so I shall turn myself over to him."

Victor shook his head vehemently. "That would be suicide."

I shrugged, "Not if you are there with me."

He took a deep breath and slowly let it out. "It could work..." his voice trailed off as he placed the blueprint on top of the desk, still staring at it.

"Of course, it will work," I said with more confidence than I actually felt. But it made sense: if we could at least gain access to the building, then I could find Daniel and he could find Espy."

Victor followed my train of thought. "But we still need to study this. We need to figure out how to get out."

I nodded, agreeing. "Then let's get to it," I announced as I sat down on the bed.

We were in for a long day and night.

CHAPTER TWENTY-FOUR

We spent the next 12 hours formulating our plan, which I felt was still far too long to wait. I was anxious about what Gabriel might do to his brother and I could feel time passing by quickly with each tick of the clock that sat beside the hotel bed.

While I studied blueprints and scribbled notes about the Knights of Christ, Victor turned the bathroom into a makeshift lab, where he built a small cyanide bomb. That was part of our escape plan, as well as a small pistol that I placed into my handbag.

Eventually, though, we were ready to follow through. Although time was of the essence, I still insisted on going back to my apartment for a quick change of clothes. If I planned on offering myself up in exchange for Daniel, I wanted to look good while doing it.

In the meantime, Victor used his network to leave word for the Knights that he would soon deliver me to them.

Victor changed and met me there. He wore slacks and a simple short-sleeved shirt, a golf cap decorating the platinum locks on his head. There was a red decorative Templar cross pinned to his shirt, a symbol that should gain us entry into the organization's building. He carefully placed the small cyanide bomb, which was no bigger than my index finger, into his front pants pocket.

Victor drove us to our destination. The city was warmer than usual, even for July. Exhaust fumed all around us, causing beads of sweat to form on the back of my neck. I dabbed at my face with a handkerchief and reapplied my lipstick and powder as we rode.

The red brick warehouse sat at the edge of the River Liffey about a 10-minute drive from downtown Dublin. I was surprised at how small it seemed when we turned into a large empty lot that led to it. I knew, though, from reviewing the blueprints that there were a series of rooms beneath the building's first floor, which hid the main base of operations of the Knights in Dublin.

Victor parked the car around the back of the building, the only vehicle there. We exited the car and approached a bright red door. Victor grabbed my arm roughly, all part of our plan, and knocked a series of taps, a code he learned that was necessary to gain entrance into the building.

A wooden panel slid from the door's surface. From behind it, two eyes with angry eyebrows stared back at us.

Victor pulled on my arm, nearly causing me to stumble. He was posing as a member of the group, with me as his prisoner.

I closed my eyes and prayed to any deity that would listen that our ruse would work.

The dark disembodied eyes scrutinized us, his gaze settling on the cross pinned to Victor's shirt and then on me. The panel slid closed, followed by the sound of disengaging locks. The door swung open and we finally saw the man attached to the angry eyebrows. He was burly with dark hair, someone we would not want to cross. "Welcome, friend," he said, although his voice was anything but welcoming. He did not look at me again. "Nom nobis. Domine, non nobis, sed nomini tuo da gloriam."

Latin was just one of the many languages that I understood. His words translated into "Not unto us, O Lord, not unto us, but unto your name, grant glory." It was a Templar slogan, one most would think long forgotten.

Victor repeated the words and bowed.

The man closed the door behind us, re-engaging the locks. He gestured to a set of stairs that led into the bowels of the building. "Take her to Gabriel."

Victor nodded and began towards the stairs, as if he visited this building regularly. Thanks to the blueprints, we both knew where to go. He roughly shoved me in front of him and towards the stairwell, forcing me to nearly trip over the top step.

"Hmmmph," the man guarding the door mumbled.

We quietly descended, certain that hidden eyes were upon us. There were cameras everywhere, making sure that we would not do anything untoward.

Several flights of stairs later, we finally found the floor of our destination. There, a long hallway spread out before us.

Victor, still holding my arm, pulled me down the hallway behind him, past dozens of rooms, finally stopping at the last one on the right of the long corridor. A door sat there, its edges illuminated from a light behind it.

"Are you ready?" Victor whispered.

I gave a quick nod and then braced myself. I knew that Gabriel, the boy - now a man - who hated me, was behind that door.

Victor knocked three times on its wooden surface.

"Enter," a voice from within said.

Victor swung the door open slowly, revealing a room swimming in reds and mahoganies. Every wooden surface gleamed, as if freshly waxed. A large elaborate desk sat at the far end of the room. Behind that desk sat a man who slightly resembled David and Daniel. This was the adult Gabriel.

Although electric light illuminated the room, several lit candles on the desk flickered, casting shadows on the walls.

"And so I have you at last," Gabriel said as he stood up and clasped his hands in front of him. He smiled and although the expression seemed to cover his face, there was no joy in what I saw there. This was someone eternally tormented with revenge and a lust for power.

This was the boy I once wanted to love me.

A door to the left of the room opened. Daniel stumbled through, followed by a gun pointed at his head held by a man standing behind him. Daniel looked disheveled, but otherwise unharmed. I let out a breath at seeing him again.

"Reine," he whispered, almost as if he did not believe I was really there.

I managed a soft smile, as if to let him know that everything was okay.

The man behind Daniel used his free hand to push Daniel to

the other side of the room. Behind them, Espy entered, another pistol attached to the hand of another man behind her.

"Oh, look, here we are all together again," Gabriel announced with a sly smile, holding his arms open. "One big happy family." He dropped his arms, but his expression did not change. "But I'm afraid that one of you has to go." He looked from Daniel to me and then to Espy.

Victor moved slowly to my right, towards Espy. No one seemed to notice him or realize that he did not belong.

"But let's make it a fair game, shall we?" Gabriel asked, tapping his fingertips against the top of the desk. "I think I'll let you choose, darling stepmother." He looked straight at me.

I saw madness behind his eyes.

Defiant, I jutted out my chin and said nothing.

Gabriel motioned to the man holding Daniel hostage. The man responded by placing the pistol's tip into Daniel's hair.

"So, which will it be, Madame?" Gabriel asked. "Will you save my brother?"

Gabriel looked at the man guarding Espy.

The man responded by grabbing her by the throat with his arm, the pistol pressed into her forehead.

"Or your daughter?" Gabriel asked.

I knew that this time I could not remain silent. My choice was clear. In fact, it was not really a choice at all. I would betray my own flesh and blood and choose Daniel. But I took my time in answering, giving Victor enough time to prepare for what happened next.

Gabriel, though, was hardly a patient man. "I'll choose for you." He gestured to the man holding Espy. The pistol next to her forehead fired.

My ears rang. I saw the gaping wound in Espy's head. She slumped down, her mouth in an "O" as if surprised. She slid to the floor, her blood staining the wooden floors.

Victor rushed to her side, all pretense lost, the bomb forgotten. He fell down beside his daughter, his face stricken with grief.

"Well, that's no fun," Gabriel said as he walked across the room towards Daniel, holding out his hand for the pistol that

Daniel's guard carried. "Maybe I should kill you, too," he said, addressing his brother.

"No!" I shouted as I reached into my purse for my gun, flinging it out in my hand, tossing my bag aside. I quickly aimed the weapon in Gabriel's general direction, but fired away from him, using the noise as a distraction. I could not risk hitting Daniel.

The shot went wild as Gabriel screamed in frustration.

In the ensuing chaos, Daniel elbowed his captor in the stomach. The man struggled, but dropped his gun in the process. Gabriel swung at his brother, but Daniel ducked the punch and fell towards the desk, which rocked underneath his weight.

Two candles fell over, setting the papers on the desk on fire.

"No! No! No!" Gabriel screamed as he started stripped off his jacket and attempted to battle the blaze with it. "Fire! Help!" he called out.

Daniel stood up and ran towards me, grabbing my hand. We made for the door that led to the outside corridor.

Gabriel looked like a demon from behind the desk, which was now completely ablaze. The fire spread quickly and eventually began to singe the furniture and bookcases, engulfing everything in its flames.

I looked over my shoulder at Victor who threw himself over Espy's lifeless body, sobbing. Fire blazed all around him and yet he seemed not to feel its heat.

I paused for only a moment, allowing myself to understand the choice I made in leaving my family behind. But then Daniel and I ran out of the door, smoke billowing behind us. The other Knights seemed so wrapped up in the fire that they ran past us, not realizing that two of their prisoners planned to escape. We ran up the stairs to the entrance, now unguarded. It took very little time to undo its series of locks. We ran out of the building, still holding hands, not stopping until we reached the edge of the river.

I heard the sound of the fire brigade arriving on the scene, but I paid it no mind.

Instead, I looked at Daniel and he looked at me. We were safe. We were alive.

Daniel brought his face closer to mine, his fingertips cupping my chin.

This time, I did not pull away.

When our lips met, the world became solid again, full of color and life.

That kiss was not just our first, but also our last.

We hailed a taxi that took us home, but once there, Daniel went to our room. I followed and watched as he pulled out a suitcase and began to pack his clothes and other things. I stared at him, confused, wondering if I should do the same.

But then he explained. "I'm so sorry, Reine, but I must leave." He took clothes out of his bureau and carefully folded them before placing them in the case. He worked methodically, although I noticed that his hands shook.

I stood in the doorway, leaning against the frame as if that would keep me from falling over. I felt as if the wind had left my body, leaving me without oxygen, without words. I could not make sense of what he said.

Had I not just saved him? Had I not just kissed him? Had I not just professed my love for him? Had I not shown him that he meant more to me than my own daughter?

It did not make sense.

Daniel continued his attempt at an explanation. "While I was in that prison," he shook his head as if ridding himself of bad memories. "I had time to think, to reflect. And do you know what I realized?"

I shook my head slowly, as tears began to slide down my pristine face. I felt a myriad of emotions come over me: fear, anger and sadness combined enough that I very nearly screamed at him as loudly as my vocal cords would allow.

This was unexpected. This was certainly not wanted.

And still, he kept speaking. He kept breaking my heart.

"I realized that I have only ever been under your care," he said. His voice was low and the words pained him. "And that I have never gone out and discovered the world on my own. You have always been there, Reine. Protecting me. I am grateful for that, I am..." He stopped packing and turned to face me, his face screwed up in angst. "I am so grateful."

A sob caught in my throat as our eyes met. I saw that he was serious. I felt my knees turn to jelly, but I clung to the edge of the door frame, forcing myself to remain standing.

He walked towards me.

I wanted to move away, but I could not. Because if I moved, I would surely faint.

He took my hands in his and lifted one palm up to his lips. He kissed it, sending a tingle of warmth up my arm and into my heart.

His actions did not align with his words.

"I love you, Reine," he whispered. "But I need to go out into the world alone. I need to learn how to be my own man."

I heard his words, but my mind continued to argue with them as he held my hands. How could this man who loved me so much now tell me that he planned on leaving me? Perhaps I even knew that he was right. But in that moment, I did not care. I felt betrayed.

I finally found my voice, although it trembled as I spoke. "Why now?" It was a plea, practically begging him to change his mind.

Daniel dropped my hands, cleared his throat and returned to his packing. He did not look at me again. "Because if I don't go now," he said, "I never will." He placed a pair of shoes in the suitcase on top of his clothes and closed the lid shut. He picked the case up by its handle and looked down.

I stayed in the doorway, as if that would block his exit, as if that would keep him from going away. Even if I knew that I should support his decision to try and Become his own person.

He stood in front of me, waiting. "We will see each other again," he promised. "There is nothing that could keep us apart forever."

My heart folded in on itself and turned to ice. I did not want to believe him. Perhaps this is what I deserved. I was always the one doing the leaving, but now I was the one being left. It seemed like some kind of divine justice.

I stepped aside. "Just go," I whispered. I turned my head away. I did not want to look at him ever again.

I heard his footsteps as he walked by me and through the apartment. I heard the door open and close as the man I loved walked out of my life.

CHAPTER TWENTY-FIVE

I would not stay in Dublin without Daniel. I became a woman adrift, carelessly wandering all over the earth, eventually crossing the great Atlantic to discover the New World. The New World was old by then, of course, but it held wonders for me that distracted me from the realization that I was utterly alone.

Years passed, as they do. I flitted from city to city, from town to town, running from or searching for anything to distract me from loneliness. Instead, I only found the need to keep moving, becoming a vagabond in a world where most would settle and put down roots.

In the early days of my travels, Daniel often sent me letters, at least when he could locate me. I would respond as I could, detailing my adventures and always signing them "With Love, Reine."

Daniel, too, traveled the world. More often than not, we possibly kept missing each other. He promised that we would reunite soon, but of course, as happens, we never did.

Eventually, even the postcards with just a few sentences from Daniel stopped arriving and I lost touch with him completely.

As always, I guarded my heart carefully and did not allow myself to grieve. I was an immortal being and my long life taught me a valuable lesson: human emotion can become one's downfall. So I locked everything I had ever felt behind a carefully crafted visage and appearance.

I never loved again. I took lovers, of course, but they were flings, one night stands, the kind of affairs where I would leave as soon as the lovemaking was over, not even waiting until the next morning for breakfast. I protected my heart, but perhaps I also saved myself for the one I still hoped would find me again.

And yet he didn't. I dreamed of him often, but those dreams only left me feeling annoyed and frustrated with each passing day.

I finally got tired of running, but it seemed that the Knights of Christ were forever on my heels. David mentioned them in his early letters, too, and it seemed that they would not rest until they tracked us both down and destroyed us completely.

But in America, I found some sense of peace. I finally allowed myself to rest in the lovely town of Savannah, Georgia. I fell in love with its green squares and antebellum houses. It had an old world charm, although it was quite modern, at least to my ancient European eyes. Savannah's people were charming and kind and the small city welcomed me with open arms.

I began to live again, however guarded, although this time it was without the love of my life or a family. Although I was not very social, I began enjoying the quiet things I once did: enjoying art, reading, discussing philosophy and going to the theatre.

As years passed without any sign or word of the Knights, I became bolder, going out more often. I felt safe again, for the first time in decades. I did not make friends easily, but I started reaching out for support, for allies. This time, though, I chose to befriend the voodoo priests and priestesses of the city, those people who seemed to know me for what I was. I did not necessarily believe in magic, but they made for good confidantes and sometimes offered sacrifices in my name of villains needing punishment. They would often help me get rid of my kills, dumping the bodies in wetlands outside of the city.

I did not go hungry in Savannah. America treated me well.

Twenty years passed without incident, but I knew that would not last. It was 1983 when one of my allies came to me to warn me about a group of men who described themselves as vampire hunters. These men were in the city, asking questions about me and Daniel.

Once more, danger lurked around every corner.

But I was tired of running, so I took other precautions. I dyed my beautiful golden hair to a dull brown. When I went out, I often wore sunglasses and a hat to conceal my identity. I lived under an assumed name. My priests and priestesses offered up incantations of protection and threatened to cast curses on anyone who would harm me.

Several weeks passed like this, and constantly looking over my shoulder took its toll.

I was so very tired. I went out less with each passing day, until the day came when I knew that I would never leave my house again.

And eventually, they found me.

My time has come.

As I look out the window and down onto the street that runs in front of my dwelling, they stand there, shadows sent to taunt me, deadly intent seeping from their forms.

I should flee, I tell myself, but I do nothing. What good would more running do? I know that they would find me, no matter what. If not them, then someone else, perhaps their sons. Or their sons' sons. I have enjoyed a long life, but I do not want to spend the rest of it running. So instead, I sit here, on the corner of my four-poster bed and I wait.

Downstairs, I hear the sound of the front door being forced open. I hear footsteps in the foyer.

I write these words in my journal, in hopes that someone will see it. I try to remember to take a breath - it could be my last. If death takes me tonight, I do not welcome it, but I do accept it.

The footsteps progress to the stairs, their feet heavy, announcing their presence.

I will face *le morte* with dignity and grace.

I hear whispers at my door. The knob begins to turn.

My name is Jeanne "Reinette" Antoinette Poisson, Madame de Pompadour. The story of my life is written in blood. The shadows have found me. Let it be known that I lived, mistress to a King, marquise and vampire. I have killed many. I regret nothing.

Au revoir, mes amies...

- **Reinette Poisson, June 15, 1983**

About the Author

Robin Burks is an entertainment and science/technology writer, published author, avid con-goer and cosplayer. She has written about pop culture and entertainment for Screen Rant, The Things and FanGirlConfessions.com.

Robin is also the author of a series of speculative fiction novels: Zeus, Inc.; The Curse of Hekate; and Return of The Titans. In 2014, Indie Reader named the protagonist of that series, Alex Grosjean, as one of its Top Five Smart, Strong and Relatable Female Characters. The series was also inducted into the 2018 Darrell Awards Coger Hall of Fame.

Robin, who currently lives in Missouri with her five cats, loves all things French and has a serious obsession with Doctor Who.

Curious about other Crossroad Press books?
Stop by our site:
http://store.crossroadpress.com
We offer quality writing
in digital, audio, and print formats.

Enter the code FIRSTBOOK
to get 20% off your first order from our store!
Stop by today!